INTERDIM
EXPLORER

*For my annoying Big Brother, and all those carefree
childhood days running wild on our estate.
From your annoying Little Sister*

First published in Great Britain 2023 by Farshore
An imprint of HarperCollins*Publishers*
1 London Bridge Street, London SE1 9GF

farshore.co.uk

HarperCollins*Publishers*
Macken House, 39/40 Mayor Street Upper, Dublin 1, D01 C9W8, Ireland

Text copyright © Lorraine Gregory 2023
Illustration copyright © Jo Lindley 2023
The moral rights of the author and illustrator have been asserted.

ISBN 978 0 00 850823 4
Printed and bound in the UK using 100% renewable electricity at CPI Group (UK) Ltd

1

A CIP catalogue record for this title is available from the British Library.

Stay safe online. Any website addresses listed in this book are correct at the time
of going to print. However, Farshore is not responsible for content hosted by
third parties. Please be aware that online content can be subject to change
and websites can contain content that is unsuitable for children.
We advise that all children are supervised when using the internet.

MIX
Paper from
responsible sources
FSC™ C007454

This book is produced from independently certified FSC™ paper
to ensure responsible forest management.

For more information visit: www.harpercollins.co.uk/green

Illustrated by
JO LINDLEY

LORRAINE GREGORY

INTERDIMENSIONAL EXPLORERS

Farshore

PROLOGUE

My grandad always had a special gift for finding things that were lost.

When I was little and one of my toys would disappear, I'd tell my grandad and within a day or so he'd turn up with a big smile on his face, the missing item safely tucked in his pocket.

"But how did you find it?" I'd demand every time.

"Can't tell you that, Danny boy," he'd say, ruffling my hair. "It's top secret."

"PLEASE!" I'd beg, hanging off his arm.

And then he'd bend over and whisper in my ear.

"It's magic my lad, just a little bit of magic."

"Can I do it too?" I wanted to know.

"Maybe one day," he'd say and there was a twinkle in his eye that almost made me believe it was true.

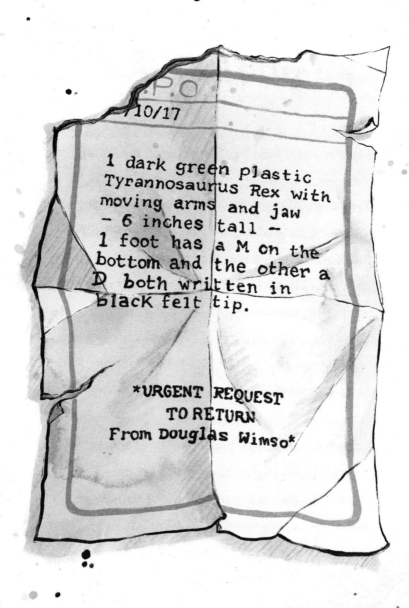

.P.O

/10/17

1 dark green plastic
Tyrannosaurus Rex with
moving arms and jaw
– 6 inches tall –
1 foot has a M on the
bottom and the other a
D both written in
black felt tip.

*URGENT REQUEST
TO RETURN
From Douglas Wimso*

CHAPTER 1

"You are in SO much trouble!" My cousin Inaaya informs me with obvious joy when she opens MY front door to let me into MY house.

"Urgh. What are you doing here?" I demand, pushing my way past her, dumping my school bag in a corner and grabbing a bag of Wotsits from the kitchen.

Inaaya follows me. "I wish I knew. Mum made me come with her even though I've got SO much homework to do, you've no idea!"

I roll my eyes and cram a handful of delicious cheesy Wotsits into my mouth.

Inaaya is always banging on about homework, just so she can remind everyone that she won a scholarship to a private school last year.

Like anyone cares.

"Wow. What a massive tragedy for you," I mutter, pouring myself a glass of water and swigging it down.

"I know!" She leans back against the wall. Despite it being the end of the day her posh school uniform looks like it's just been ironed, her long black hair is entirely contained in a neat plait and even her stupid white socks are pulled up.

"Still," she says with a wicked glint in her eye. "Watching you getting yelled at might make it worth my while, I suppose."

"What are you on about?" I ask finally.

Inaaya makes a smug face. She loves holding her knowledge over me like an evil supervillain and dragging out every second.

"Your grandad rang," she says at last and a heavy stone of dread thunks into my stomach because I've just remembered where I should have been this afternoon. "He wanted to know where you were and your mum said she thought you were working with him so then SHE rang the school and found out YOU were in detention instead!"

I swear under my breath. Getting told off is bad enough without having Inaaya here to witness it. She's the perfect child and I'm just . . . not. Not perfect, not clever and not well behaved.

I gave up even trying to keep up with her years ago when I was the only other kid at her super lame birthday party and all her presents were textbooks and school equipment. I mean, what sort of life is that?

"Danny? Is that you?" Mum's voice calls to me from the front room.

I finish my water and put the glass down.

"Better not keep her waiting!" Inaaya sings and I accidentally stamp on her foot as I march past, enjoying the crunch of her toes under my shoe and her yelp of pain.

"Danny!" My aunt Rekha cries, standing up when she sees me and opening her bangled arms wide. "Come give your auntie a hug!"

Happy to delay the inevitable telling off from Mum, I let her squeeze me for way longer than I usually would. When I eventually step back, she grabs my face in both hands and shoves my cheeks together till I look like a fish.

"Such a handsome boy!" she says and I can't help puffing my chest out a teeny bit. "If only you would brush your hair and tuck your shirt in!"

My chest deflates and I wiggle away so I can face Mum and get it over with.

"Your grandad rang," she says, eyeing me over the top of her mug of tea.

"Yeah, I know." I gulp. "Look, I'm . . ."

Mum cuts me off. "Best hurry over there now, my dad's been working much too hard lately and it sounds like he needs your help."

I'm startled into silence. Why isn't she shouting at me for lying to her and getting into trouble at school? Why isn't she moaning about how I don't work hard enough and wishing I'd "just try a bit harder because look how well your cousin Inaaya has done"?

I glance at Inaaya and her disappointed face almost makes me laugh.

"Right, yeah, I'll go over there now then," I say quickly, before she can change her mind. Maybe Mum will shout at me later but at least Inaaya won't be there to witness it.

"Oh . . . wait," Mum says, as her gaze drifts away to meet Aunt Rekha's for a moment. "Can you take your cousin with you, please. Give us a bit of peace to catch up properly."

I groan silently. I might have known Mum would find a way to punish me somehow.

"Er, no, it's all right, Auntie Leanne," Inaaya says quickly. "Danny should go and see his grandad on his own. I'll stay here. I've got homework to get on with."

"Yeah, see, Inaaya has homework," I add, feeling a teeny smidge of gratitude to Inaaya. There's no way Mum will be able to argue against homework!

"The fresh air will do you good, beta," Aunt Rekha says, tucking her bare feet under her on the sofa and dunking a biscuit in her tea. "Go with your cousin. Your aunt and I have a few important things to discuss."

"Of course, Mum." Inaaya kisses her mum on the cheek and waits politely for me to move.

I huff down the hallway with my perfect cousin

hanging on my heels like an annoyingly well-groomed dog and head out on to the estate.

Inaaya doesn't say anything as we walk but her shoulders are hunched up near her ears and she keeps glancing around her all the time like she's being followed.

"What's up with you?" I ask. "Sad 'cos you missed out on seeing me get in trouble?"

"Nothing's up with me," she says, jumping at the random slam of a car door.

"What? Do you think you're gonna get mugged or something?"

She shrugs. "It's not my fault your estate has a bad reputation."

I grind my teeth. Honestly, just because it's a council estate doesn't mean it's dangerous! It's more like a big family, somewhere you can belong, somewhere you feel safe.

"That's fake news, Inaaya. No one's going to mug you!"

However, I am considering whether it's possible to accidentally lose her somewhere . . . I mean, it would be easy enough. My estate is MASSIVE and if you don't grow up here it's almost impossible to find your way around. I reckon if I'm clever she might not turn up again till Christmas.

I hurry her through one of the garage blocks that line the far edge of the estate and across the concrete "playground". I turn left past the block of flats where my best mate Modge lives and then swing right down an overgrown, rubbish-strewn alley to try and lose her.

But no such luck.

Inaaya stays glued to my heels the whole way to my grandad's block, and follows me up the concrete steps to the first floor.

I really hope my grandad's not too annoyed about me being late. I hate it when he's upset with me. I've been helping him out a fair bit lately 'cos it's a lot of work being caretaker on an estate this size and Mum was worried it was getting a bit too much for him.

I'd promised to help with setting up this new batch of smoke alarms today, but then I got this stupid detention from Mr Ossard for something I didn't even

do and I forgot to ring him and now it's all a big mess.

"Urgh! What's that smell?" Inaaya demands, wrinkling up her nose.

"I can't smell anything," I insist, which isn't exactly true. All the stairways pong of wee a bit if I'm honest, but I hardly notice it any more. They're still fun to mess about in. The whole estate is good for that, actually. There's so many alleyways and ramps and balconies and sheds that me and Modge never get bored.

But Modge isn't here. Instead I've got Little Miss Boring trailing behind me down the balcony to my grandad's flat, with one hand dramatically clamped to her nostrils.

I knock on the door a few times but there's no answer, so I peer through the letter box.

"GRANDAD!" I yell because he's a bit deaf now and doesn't always hear me.

There's still no answer.

"What now?" Inaaya asks with a long-suffering sigh.

"He must be at the workshop already," I tell Inaaya, a squirrel of guilt scurrying around my gut because he'd have had to carry all the smoke alarms over there by himself and there were loads of them. "It's not far, don't worry."

"I'm not worried."

"You look worried."

"Well, I'm not." She hurries back down the hall.

"Good, because it's perfectly safe here," I call after her. "Just 'cos we're poor doesn't mean we're all criminals, you know."

"I never said you ALL were!" she snaps.

"Good!"

"Just most of you," she adds, under her breath.

"That is SO not true! Most people here are really nice!" And definitely WAY more fun than the miserable, snotty neighbours who live in her fancy cul-de-sac.

"Oy!" Keylon "Bully" Molloy pipes up out of nowhere, as if he was hanging around, just waiting to prove me wrong. "Where do you think you're going, Danny Dourado?"

He's planted himself right between us and the landing, arms crossed, trouble written all over his face. His brother Sags is behind him, trying to look menacing. They're not exactly criminals but the Molloy family are definitely in training.

"What do you want?" I demand.

Keylon holds out his hand. "Gotta pay a toll if you want to get past."

"A toll? Get stuffed!"

"What?" he says, leering at Inaaya. "Your posh little girlfriend looks like she's got a few quid."

"She's NOT my girlfriend!" I tell him. "And we're not giving you any money. Just move."

I stand my ground and try not to let my knees wobble. Keylon is two years older and three inches taller than me. In a fight he'd flatten me. I know that. And he knows that. But if I give in just once he'll never stop bullying me, will he? And besides, I can't let Inaaya see me get pushed about on my own estate.

"I'm not going anywhere and neither are you two!" Keylon snarls.

"Yeah!" Sags agrees, always super brave when he's hiding behind one of his older brothers.

My brain starts frantically working out a plan, but I don't think magically learning to fly is going to happen somehow.

"This is a free country! I demand you let me pass," Inaaya says, glaring at Keylon and making everything about fifty times worse.

Keylon and Sags snort with laughter.

"Ooh! Get her!" Keylon says, while Sags does a high-pitched impression of her voice that makes them laugh even harder.

"SHUT UP, YOU IGNORANT NEANDERTHALS!" Inaaya yells, her fists clenched in rage. I can just tell this is NOT going to end well.

"All right!" I shout over the noise they're making. "I'll give you a quid, Keylon, just let us pass."

"Danny!" Inaaya hisses. "You can't reward this sort of behaviour!"

I ignore her and show Keylon my last pound coin.

Keylon shoots Inaaya a smug look and holds his hand out. I press the coin into his palm and he moves aside.

I grab Inaaya's arm and pull her quickly down the stairs behind me while she mutters about me being a coward.

"Oy!" Sags shouts over the balcony. "This isn't a pound! It's a poxy swimming locker token!"

"You're welcome!" I yell back. Serves them right for not noticing when I switched the coins.

"You just wait, Danny Dourado! We'll get you and your stupid little girlfriend!" Keylon promises.

"SHE'S NOT MY GIRLFRIEND!" I yell back but they're not on the balcony any more. They're coming after us!

CHAPTER 2

I take off running, whipping past two blocks of flats and through the garages as quick as I can. I hide behind the stinky bin sheds for a second to see if the Molloys are coming and when the coast is clear I run down an alleyway, past the broken sheds, round to the estate shop and . . .

"Stop!" Inaaya gasps. "I can't breathe!"

She bends over, panting and holding her side.

I fold my arms and sniff. "I thought all that jolly hockey-sticks stuff you play at your fancy school would keep you fit."

"Oh, shut up," she snaps, slowly straightening up. "You're the one trying to get us beaten up!"

I remind her, our close escape just sinking in. "How come you're picking fights with the Molloys when you're so terrified of getting mugged?"

"Those idiots aren't dangerous, they're just stupid bullies and you can't give in to bullies," she insists, flicking her plait back over her shoulder.

I don't know what sort of bullies she's met before but the Molloys are dangerous enough, if you ask me. They're always prowling the estate, spoiling other kids' fun and causing trouble.

"You should be more careful who you mess with round here," I tell her.

"I thought you said it was perfectly safe on your precious estate!"

"Well, it is! Mostly. Apart from the Molloys."

Inaaya stands up straight again and rolls her eyes at me. "Well, I'm glad you didn't give those imbeciles any money."

"And I'm glad they didn't catch us. Mum would only blame me if you got thumped."

Inaaya sniffs and looks around. "How much further is it?"

"It's just over there."

I point out the large building set at the far edge

of the estate where my grandad has his office and workshop. It's his job to do maintenance on the estate and fix things that break, which keeps him pretty busy because with council houses things are ALWAYS breaking. Luckily, he's got me to help him out. When I'm not in detention, obviously.

I pull open the door to Grandad's office, which is basically an old Portakabin, and go inside. His desk is super tidy as always. The heavy old-fashioned typewriter takes up about half of it. The massive black telephone, with the message light flashing, takes up the other half.

"Wow. It's like a time warp in here," Inaaya says.

"Yeah. My grandad doesn't trust technology." I've told him to get a computer and a smartphone to make his life easier, but he won't.

"I thought you said he'd be here?"

I shrug. "He'll be in his workshop."

I step through the back door into the cavernous room behind.

"GRANDAD!" I yell and it echoes around the space for ages.

No answer.

I walk past heaving shelves of old parts and his workbench full of half-finished jobs. The smell of glue and oil fills my nose and takes me right back to being five again and playing at my grandad's feet while he fixed something or other.

"Grandad! It's me, Danny! Sorry I'm late!" I shout again, wondering where he's got to. He's not out on a job because his worn leather tool belt is still hanging up on the hook and he never goes to work without that.

I'm nearly at the back when I see a light: a strange

blue light that hurts my eyes.

"GRANDAD! WHERE ARE YOU?"

I start to hurry towards the light. I don't know why exactly, but my heart is thumping and I can feel the hairs on my arms standing up.

Then I see him. Bathed in a prism of blue light and lurching out of one of the old, battered lockers behind him.

"Grandad?"

He staggers out, into the workshop, and the blue light from the locker vanishes. He makes it a few steps, lets out a cry of pain, clutches his right arm and then falls backwards on to the ground, not moving.

My brain stutters for a long moment, trying to make sense of what's happened. Then a spike of panic takes over and I run to his side, kneel down and pat his face.

"Grandad? Can you hear me? It's Danny. Are you all right?"

His eyes are closed but I can see his chest rise and fall so I know he's still alive, at least. Whatever's wrong with him must be bad, though. Really bad. Because he looks awful. All sweaty and pale.

"What's wrong with him?" Inaaya asks, skidding to

a halt a few feet away, her voice high with fear.

"I don't know." My eyes are stinging with tears but I swipe them away before Inaaya can see. "Call an ambulance! Quick!"

She digs in her blazer pocket for her phone and taps away at it. "It's not working! I don't understand."

"The signal in here is rubbish. Use the landline in the office!" I shout.

"Okay. I'll be back in a minute!" She turns and runs off.

"Grandad? Please say something?" I'm trying desperately to remember what it said on that first aid video they made us watch at school but I can't. I can't think of anything except how scared I am.

He twitches, moans, tries to sit up then collapses back on the ground. One eye opens and he peers at me.

"Grandad! You're all right!" The hard ache under my ribs eases a little.

"Danny?"

"I'm here." I yank my jumper off, pad it up and gently ease it under his head.

". . . thought you weren't coming . . ." His voice is

really weak and I'm so scared because I've never seen him sick or hurt before and for the first time ever he actually seems old. My gut twists with guilt because I should have been here. I should have been helping him like I promised.

"It's all right, I'm here now," I tell him, hating myself for getting a stupid detention when he needed me. "We're getting help, an ambulance is coming."

Grandad opens his eyes and grips my hand hard. "Listen to me now, Danny . . . it's very important."

"What is?"

"I need you to do something . . . you have to help me."

"Anything," I insist.

"I need you to be caretaker now . . ."

"What?" I frown. "But I can't do plumbing and stuff on my own, Grandad. I'm just a kid!"

"Not here . . . there."

"What do you mean? Where?"

"Take this key." He taps at his top pocket. I reach in but the only thing in there is his old watch on a chain. I pull it out anyway. "Go through to the office . . ." He pauses, swallows.

"The office?" I glance towards the Portakabin.

"Not that one," he says. "There . . ."

His hand lifts and points at the locker.

"But . . . that's just a locker, Grandad!"

"No . . . it's not. Listen, I'm sorry, not to tell you before, but . . . there are many worlds out there, Danny . . . many worlds . . ."

I frown and shake my head. What's he on about? Many worlds? In a locker?! He must be confused. Maybe he hurt his head when he fell?

"It's all right, Grandad, calm down."

"PROMISE ME!" He jerks upright, staring right into my eyes. "Promise you'll go to the office and look after them for me, keep them safe. Promise you won't let me down! I know you can do it. You're the only one I can trust."

I'm scared he's going to die if he keeps on like this.

"All right, Grandad!" I tell him. "I promise." The watch tingles in my hand and I stuff it in my pocket quickly.

"DANNY!" he shouts again, his voice hoarse and desperate.

"What is it, Grandad?" I bend down closer.

"BEWARE THE CHEESE!" he yells in my face before coughing and collapsing back on the floor.

"Grandad?" I give his hand a hard squeeze, but his eyes stay closed and I don't think he can hear me any more.

"Danny!" Inaaya calls. "The ambulance is coming! I'll go outside and wait for them!"

I sit in the gloom and watch my grandad's chest rise and fall till the sound of the ambulance siren fills the air like a warning that everything has changed forever.

CHAPTER 3

Ever since I got home from school I've been mooching around the house like a bear in a cage. Mum and Dad are at the hospital with Grandad and I can't settle at anything. Even YouTube's enormous selection of cats' greatest jumping fails can't distract me from all the guilt and worry curdling in my belly like sour milk.

When the doorbell goes, I consider not answering it and just lying here on the sofa forever. But eventually I decide any distraction is better than none.

"All right, Danny?" Modge says, turning up just when I need him like a best mate should.

"Modge!" I grab his arm and drag him into the house. "I thought you weren't coming back from your mum's till next week?" Modge's mum works on the cruise ships as a singer, so he lives with his dad most of the time. He goes to stay with his mum a couple of times a year, whenever she's back home in England.

"Yeah . . . something came up, so I came home early," Modge says, chewing at his bottom lip and looking even more confused than usual.

I do my best to wait for more info, but with Modge that can take forever and I need to talk to someone NOW.

"Did you hear about my grandad?" I blurt.

"Yeah, Dad told me. I'm sorry, mate. How is he?"

I lead Modge into the kitchen and grab the biscuit tin. Modge snags two Jaffa cakes and a hobnob and stuffs them in his mouth one after the other. He eats non-stop but you'd never tell, seeing as he's skinny as a pole. He's also got funny yellow hair that sticks up in odd places, one wonky tooth (from an epic skateboarding fail that I'm not allowed to mention EVER) and a birthmark on his arm shaped exactly like a dalek.

"The doctors think he'll be all right, but it was a pretty bad heart attack," I say. "They said it was lucky

I was there. If we hadn't got him to hospital straight away, he could have died."

"Wow! You saved his life, Danny!" Modge slaps me on the shoulder. Mum had hugged me hard enough to hurt when she found out and the doctor at the hospital shook my hand. They all think I did something special.

"Yeah, but this stupid detention made me late, Modge," I confess. "I promised I'd be there to help him and I wasn't. I let him down, Modge, I should have been there."

"You were there when he needed you, mate."

"Yeah . . . I suppose." But maybe if I'd been there on time he wouldn't have had a heart attack in the first place! What if this is ALL my fault?"

"He'll be all right, Danny. Your grandad's well tough," Modge says. "Remember that time he climbed up the drainpipe to rescue that little girl when there was a fire in their kitchen?"

I can't help smiling. My grandad IS a bit of a legend on our estate. They took his picture for the local paper after he saved that girl and Grandad insisted I was

Local hero, Mr Wimso (67), pictured with quick-thinking grandson, Danny (8)

in it too because I was the one who spotted the smoke and called him. Mum still has that photo of us both up on the wall. I can almost feel his strong arm around me even now, keeping me safe – keeping everyone safe.

He is tough, my grandad. I know that, but Modge didn't see him yesterday looking all sick and old.

"Yeah, I know . . . but he was acting well weird when I found him."

"So would you if your heart stopped beating!"

"No. I mean REALLY weird," I say. "He kept saying something about wanting me to go to an office in a locker and look after them. He didn't say what 'them' was exactly, but he did say there were many worlds out there or something."

Modge snorts. "Had he been drinking? My great aunt Edna talks like that after she's been on the sherry at Christmas."

"No, he never drinks," I insist. "And there was this light, Modge. A strange blue light coming from the locker. And the really weird thing is, he stepped OUT of that locker, Modge, just before he fell down. I saw him. I mean, what was he doing INSIDE a locker in the first place?"

"Well, you can ask him when he's better."

"Yeah . . . but he made me promise," I tell him, feeling the weight of it pressing on my shoulders.

"Promise what?" Modge asks.

"To go there and protect them."

"Go to the office in the locker?"

"Yep." I glance at Modge, trying to work out if he believes me.

Modge crams another biscuit in his mouth, sticks two more in his pocket and stands up. "Come on then."

"What?"

"You're not going to stop worrying about it till we go and look, so let's just go and look now."

"You don't think I'm mad?"

"Well, course I do!" says Modge. "But mad or not, you're still my best mate, aren't you?"

That's what I like about Modge. He's brutally honest but loyal to the end.

"Ooh, it's well spooky in here," Modge whispers when we walk into the silent gloom of the empty workshop.

"Why are you whispering?" I whisper.

"Why are YOU whispering?" he whispers back.

"I dunno," I whisper, but it almost feels like we're trespassing being here without my grandad. This is HIS place, where he was at his most happy pottering around fixing things for other people . . .

I take a deep breath. It's going to be okay. He's going to be back home soon, that's what Mum said on the phone, and I'm going to prove he can rely on me by doing exactly what he asked for once.

"Come on!" I hurry round to the back where the lockers are standing against the wall.

"That's them? Really?" Modge asks with a disappointed frown.

I can't blame him for doubting. The lockers look perfectly normal. Just tall grey metal things, like you'd find in a school or gym, all battered and old with graffiti and stickers all across them.

"I know," I admit. "This is mad, isn't it?"

"But you saw a light, right? And your grandad coming out?"

"Yeees . . . but maybe I was in shock or something?" I suggest. "I mean, why would anyone come out of a locker?"

"Just open it and see!" Modge instructs.

I take a deep breath and put my hand on the door.

"What if there's an alien monster inside?" I ask Modge.

"Then we make friends with it and get him to stomp on the Molloys!" Modge says. "Now just open it!"

"All right, all right," I grumble. It's fine for him. He's standing well out of the way. I'M the one who'll get shot by the alien's poxy plasma rifle!

I jerk the door open and try and duck at the same time just in case.

It doesn't go very well and I end up slamming the door into my head instead.

Modge's laughter echoes all around me.

"Classic!" he shouts. "Do it again so I can catch it on my phone!"

"No! Ow! I might have concussion or something!" I press my hand to my forehead. I'm sure there's a bruise. Honestly. I'm such an idiot. The door swings harmlessly open and there's no aliens. No blue light. Nothing at all.

Modge sighs and comes to check on me.

"Move your hand then," he says.

Reluctantly I shift it so he can look at my head.

"It's pretty bad, Danny."

"What?"

"Yep, your whole brain has disappeared."

"Oh ha flipping ha."

Modge pokes at the sore bit with his finger and I give him a shove. He stumbles back, trips over his own feet and starts to fall.

I try and catch him but his panicked hands grip

my arms and I end up being dragged backwards with him instead. We both fall right inside the locker with a heavy slam – and all the air leaves my body with a whoosh.

There's a weird tingle in my jeans pocket where I put Grandad's watch and then a blue light surrounds us, so bright it hurts my eyes and hot as anything. Before I can even open my mouth to scream for help, we both fall out again in a tangle of arms and legs.

I drag in a deep breath and try and move.

"Gerroff me!" Modge says, wriggling like a demented caterpillar.

"I'm trying!" I snap, unwrapping my leg from round his waist and getting to my feet.

"Wait . . . how hard did I hit my head?" I ask, looking around slowly.

Modge's jaw drops open.

Because there's no sign of any locker, no sign of my grandad's workshop and we're not anywhere I recognise. The locker has transported us somewhere ENTIRELY different.

CHAPTER 4

"Well," Modge says, digging out one of the biscuits from his pocket and slowly munching on it. "This is a bit weird."

"A bit weird?" I choke out. "This is more than a bit flaming weird! This is massively, humungously, gigantically weird!"

Somehow we're now in a small room, painted cream with a tiled floor, a potted plant, a coffee table and a couple of plastic chairs. It's so ordinary it makes me nervous because there's something not right about it. There's something missing. Like the air isn't moving right.

Oh, and there's a tinted glass door on the opposite wall.

I walk closer so I can see the sign written on the glass.

IDLPO

"IDLPO?" I say.

"What?" Modge says.

"That's what it says on the door. IDLPO."

"What's an IDLE POO?"

"How should I know?"

Modge rubs his head. "Is it like when my dad spends an hour in the toilet on a Saturday morning reading the newspaper?"

"Urgh. No, it's not. It doesn't even say Idle POO, Modge. It says Idle PO!"

"Well, I don't know, do I? Just open the door and see."

"Why? 'Cos it worked so well last time?"

"It's not my fault you can't open a door properly," Modge points out. "If you hadn't banged your head, we wouldn't be here."

"You're the one who poked me. It's your fault we fell!"

Modge huffs. "Just open the door, Danny. Maybe it will take us back home?"

I grab the glass door's handle and pull it down hard. Nothing happens, even after I wriggle it.

"It's locked."

"You said your grandad gave you a key, didn't you?" says Modge.

"Well, he gave me his old pocket watch . . ." I dig it out of my jeans and open the silver case to check – but nope, there's no key hiding there. I don't know why he even keeps this old thing, let alone carries it around with him everywhere. It doesn't even work as a watch any more. The hands stopped moving years ago, so it's always 2.35. Still, it's heavy and warm in my hand and it feels good to have something of his with me.

"He must have given me the wrong thing," I tell Modge. "This old watch of his is definitely NOT a key!"

I poke it at the lock to prove my point. The watch makes a small chiming noise like a bell and there's a complicated clicking sound from the door.

Something makes me try the handle again. This

time the door swings open.

Swallowing hard, I step inside and stare at the large office. Shelves ring the walls and a big shiny wooden desk sits at the front. There's a fancy leather chair behind it and a massively thick book sat on top.

"Modge," I whisper as he joins me. "What is going on?"

"I dunno," says Modge. "But your grandad wasn't confused. This really IS an office and it IS in a locker."

"But what sort of office is it?" I ask. "And what's it doing in a locker? And where is HERE exactly?"

Looking at the office more closely does NOT calm me down because the light above me isn't coming from a NORMAL lightbulb, but some sort of PLANT with big glowing buds that grows across the ceiling in twirling purple vines.

And the chair looks like NORMAL leather at first but there are big dragon-like scales on it that RIPPLE when I stroke them.

AND there's a goldfish bowl on the shelf that has a stripy THREE-EYED fish swimming in it.

I swallow down the rising panic and walk over to the desk to take a closer look at the book on the table, hoping for answers.

"Interdimensional Lost Property Office Official Log Book" is embossed on the front of the book in silver letters. I guess that's what the IDLPO. on the door stands for. But to be fair, those words just makes me even more confused. Nervously I open it up at a random page. I can see it's my grandad's handwriting. When I flick through, it's clear that the entries go back for years. But most of it makes no sense at all.

1 Ruberous Elephus Horn - 19th December 1999 - 3651239/H - Dimension QS - shelving quadrant B.

12 Orange Flurgleton - LIVE - 21st March 2000 - 7658912/W - Dimension AXW - shelving quadrant F1 - Collected 17th Dec 2004

3 Barrels of Lightning Frogs - 3rd September 2009 - 1456289/Y Dimension Zb - shelving quadrant A99

I slam the book shut and sit down in the big leather chair, feeling slightly ill. It's like the world has tipped on its side.

"Er . . . Danny?" Modge says from behind me.

"What?"

"You might want to have a look at this."

I'm not actually sure I do. But I get up anyway and walk towards Modge, who's slid open another door at the back of the office. Beyond this door is a much bigger room, and in the middle of it there's a huge tube full of wildly swirling items all caught in some sort of sparkly blue net.

My eyes are drawn upwards to what looks like a giant black hole at the top of the net. Peering into it makes me feel all dizzy and strange.

I close my eyes, just for a second. When I open them again Modge's face is leering at me from about half a centimetre away and I very bravely scream and fall over.

"So, this is a lost property office then?" Modge says after I've thumped him in the arm and shown him the book. "My nan took me to one of them at the station once when she left her suitcase on the train. It didn't look ANYTHING like this though."

I point out the words on the cover. "This book says it's an INTERDIMENSIONAL lost property office."

"What even IS a dimension?" Modge asks.

I shrug. "No idea. But the items in this book are proper WEIRD." I flick through the pages to show him. "I mean, WHAT is a Flurgleton? That's not normal. Flurgletons don't exist on earth."

Modge frowns at me. "So you think they came from somewhere else . . . like . . . like outer space or something?"

I look around me at all the odd stuff and shrug. "Maybe? I mean, my grandad was going on about 'other worlds'. Maybe he meant other space dimensions or something."

"I'm not being funny," Modge says, "but if there were loads of other dimensions, worlds, whatever, wouldn't we have heard about it?"

I close the book and look at Modge. "Maybe no one else knows about them?"

Modge shakes his head. "But if these other

dimensions are just flinging their lost property around all over the place, how could we not know? How does all this stuff even get in here? And where does it all go?"

"I don't know!"

"Look," Modge declares, crossing his arms over his chest. "There's NO such thing as inter-wotsit lost property offices! There just isn't!"

"But unless we've both gone bonkers, then we're standing in one right now," I say. "Maybe this really is some special place for all the lost property from space?"

Modge snorts. "Come on, Danny! Why would an inter-wotsit lost property office be hidden in a manky old locker in a caretaker's workshop on a council estate in East London? And why would your grandad of all people be working here? It makes no sense."

"I don't know, Modge. He never said a word to me about ANY of this."

"What, never?"

"No! I mean . . ." An old and almost forgotten memory worms its way into my brain. "He was always really good at finding things though," I say slowly.

"Whenever I lost my toys, I'd tell him and sometimes he'd turn up with them a few days later. He used to say it was magic. But maybe THIS is what he meant. Maybe all my lost toys came here when they disappeared and he just brought them back to me."

"But why would your lost toys come here?" Modge demands.

I have no idea. But clearly Grandad DID find my toys somewhere. Maybe there really is some sort of system in place for lost stuff. But without Grandad here to explain it all, Modge and me are just wandering about in the dark without a poxy torch.

I rub my hands through my hair and try to focus. "So the important thing is doing what my grandad asked, which is looking after something. I just need to work out what."

My eyes search the floors and tables and shelves. I can't see anything that looks like it needs looking after (except for the three-eyed fish) so what was Grandad talking about? And what am I supposed to do now?

It's all too much. My head feels like it might explode if one more weird thing happens.

And then a massive blue squid with a poodle perm and a glass bowl on her head rides a purple Segway into the office.

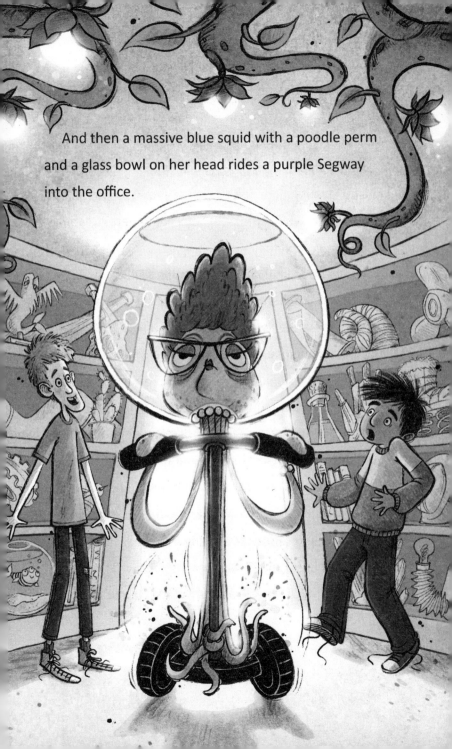

CHAPTER 5

"Cor! Are you a squid?" Modge asks, looking completely thrilled at this new arrival. He seems to be taking this whole 'fell through a locker into a magical lost property office' thing much better than me.

The squid ignores him.

"I am Mrs Arburknuckle," she says, sounding a bit like the queen but underwater. "I'm supervisor of the third district interdimensional lost property offices. Who are you? What are you doing here?"

My mouth hangs open for a minute as I just stare, trying to make sense of what my eyes are seeing.

"WELL?" the squid snaps.

"Er . . . I'm Danny," I say. "My grandad told me to come."

"Your grandad is Douglas Wimso?"

I nod.

She spins her head round a few times looking for him. "Where is he? Why has this office been inactive for so long?"

"Oh . . . er . . . well, it's because my grandad had a heart attack and he's in the hospital," I explain, trying to ignore the fact that I'm talking to a squid on a Segway.

"This is most inconvenient!" she says with a huff. "I assume you're the new caretaker?"

"Er . . ." I remember that's what Grandad called me when he gave me the key, so I nod.

"Well, make sure you get everything up and running as soon as possible."

Mild panic sets in. Get WHAT up and running?

"Yeah, right . . ." I bite my lip. "What am I supposed to do again, exactly?"

"Surely your grandfather already covered that in your training?"

Training?

She peers at me through her helmet thingy. "You did complete your training, didn't you?"

I squirm under her gaze. "Not exactly."

Mrs Arburknuckle groans and starts muttering to herself. "I might have known there'd be something!

There always is! I suppose I'll have to send in a replacement caretaker now, but who?"

For a single second I imagine just walking away, letting someone else take over and forgetting all this ever happened.

But watching her tentacles skip over a silver pad, as she tries to find a replacement for my grandad, I realise that's the last thing I want. No one can replace him. Not ever. Because he's the best grandad in the world, and if it's my fault he had a heart attack then this might be my one chance to make it up to him.

"Wait," I tell her. "Don't send in anyone else. I can do it . . . till my grandad comes back, anyway."

She squints at me. "Young man, being caretaker of an IDLPO is a very responsible job and you don't seem very responsible to me!"

"He is though, trust me!" Modge says, slinging a skinny arm round my shoulders. "And I can TOTALLY help him out."

Mrs Arburknuckle sighs. "I'd have to do your induction right now and I really don't have the time."

"Please, Mrs Arburknuckle?" I beg. "I promised my grandad."

Mrs Arburknuckle wobbles all over as she sighs, loudly. "Oh, very well. I suppose you two could manage the basic sorting, as there are no return days planned for a while. Luckily for you, this office is part of the marvellous new trial at the Hub, and you won't have to deal with any live creatures."

"Live creatures?" Modge asks, his eyes going wide cos he loves animals and is desperate for a pet of his own.

"Yes, the smaller ones do sometimes fall through –" She stops suddenly and glares at us. "Have you two signed an interdimensional secrecy order?"

I shake my head.

She flings three tentacles up in the air in frustration. "You could all be arrested, you realise? Secrecy is PARAMOUNT to our very existence!"

"Sorry."

The squid sighs. "You'll just have to sign the documents now. Come on."

"Two interdimensional secrecy orders," she says into her silver pad and the screen turns green. "Come on then. Press your hand on there."

"What for?" Modge asks because he's obviously

much braver than me.

The squid sighs. "You are merely confirming that you will not tell anyone, ever, about the IDLPO or anything that occurs while in the IDLPO, nor reveal the truth about interdimensional reality for as long as you live."

"But why do you need my hand?" I ask. "Can't I just sign it?"

"You are, by leaving your fingerprints and DNA."

"Oh."

Nervously, I press my hand on the screen and a light scans it. Before I can move it away, a sharp stab of electricity jerks through my hand and I let out a loud yelp.

"Well, how did you think we were going to get your DNA?" Mrs Arburknuckle asks.

I flap my hand around to try and get rid of the pins and needles. Modge gulps.

"It's all right, it doesn't hurt that much," I tell him, and the daft muppet actually believes me and lays his hand on the screen.

While he's yelping and jumping around, Mrs Arburknuckle puts her pad away. "Now, if you attempt to tell ANYONE else about the existence of the IDLPO, your brains will turn to mush and leak from your ears, is that clear?"

"Wait, what?" Modge says but the squid isn't listening.

"Your induction starts here. Please pay attention. You are part of an interdimensional multiverse . . ."

"What dimension are we in now then?" I ask because it seems like it might be useful information.

"Yeah, cos we fell in to this old locker in Danny's grandad's workshop and then we just ended up here!" Modge adds. "It was well weird."

"You're in the same dimension as normal. You merely passed through a doorway," Mrs A says, like that should be obvious or something.

"But this office isn't IN my grandad's workshop!" I insist. "There's just shelves and old junk in there!"

"It IS there," says Mrs Arburknuckle, "because that is the exact point where the lost property falls through. We've simply compressed this office area into a fragment of space and disguised it. The locker is just a highly secure doorway to allow the caretaker to enter the IDLPO using the key."

I frown. "But why does lost property from all these other dimensions fall into my grandad's workshop?"

"If you'll let me finish!" Mrs A snaps. "The entire multiverse is controlled and managed by Centralus – the original and central dimension from which all other dimensions are based. Centralus set up the network of lost property offices many years ago to ensure all items that come through the wyrm holes are safely logged and –"

"Ooh, I know all about worm holes!" Modge interrupts. "I saw it on Doctor Who. They're like tunnels that travel between two places in space."

Mrs A snorts. "You're talking about WORM holes but I'm referring to WYRM holes, young man. They're completely different."

She zooms through to the back room.

"Is it me or did she just say the SAME thing was a DIFFERENT thing?" I ask Modge.

"I HAVEN'T GOT ALL DAY!" Mrs A shouts before Modge can answer and we hurry after her.

"This is a WYRM hole," she says, pointing at the big hole above the blue net. "It's one of many created by the rampant Flurian wyrm many centuries ago. It tried to eat the Flurm contained in the Great Pillar which supports and links all the dimensions together."

Modge looks at me.

I look at Modge.

"You mean a REAL WORM MADE THAT HOLE?" I ask, feeling faintly sick.

"Isn't that what I just said?"

"Blimey, how big is its mouth?" Modge asks.

"I don't have time for a biology lesson on the

anatomy of the Flurian wyrm, young man. All you need to know is that occasionally items fall through the wyrm holes into other dimensions and the IDLPOs were created by Centralus to manage those items safely and avoid any dangerous situations, that's all."

"So there are more of these IDLPOs then?" I ask.

"Of course. The multiverse requires an entire network to manage all the items that fall through wyrm holes, and I run a whole department at Centralus Interdimensional Headquarters to supervise them."

Right, so my toys had fallen down one of the wyrm holes in THIS DIMENSION and ended up in an IDLPO in ANOTHER DIMENSION and then my grandad had brought them all back to me? And he'd never said a flaming word to me about dimensions or wyrms or anything!

A weird beeping starts on Mrs Arburknuckle's Segway. She tuts, reaches into her basket, pulls out her silver pad and sighs at whatever she reads. "I have to go, I'm afraid. There's a rampant Gurflungus emergency in sector Z'gnuf."

"But we still don't know what to do!" I remind her.

She peers round the office, spots something on a

shelf and uses a tentacle to retrieve it. She drops the heavy dusty book into my hand.

"Read this instruction manual. You'll have to use the translation menu in the front to pick your language until I can get hold of some language widgets for you. Everything you need to know is inside," she says, zooming towards the door on her Segway.

"Wait!" I shout, running after her. "Don't go!"

"I am EXTREMELY busy, young man, there are important things I have to deal with."

"Right, but . . ." I lower my voice to a whisper. "Is this all actually real or what?"

Mrs Arburknuckle slaps a damp tentacle into my face and waggles it about. "Does that feel real?"

"Yes," I mutter, wiping at my soggy face.

"Then let's just assume it's all real, shall we? Now I'm expecting you to deal with this horrific backlog and keep the office running smoothly until Douglas can return."

"No problem," Modge confirms. "We'll get right to work, don't worry about a thing, Mrs Squid."

With an exasperated huff she's gone, and I wonder if I was just having some sort of stress delusion.

"That Segway was totally cool!" Modge says, making it all real again. "Do you think we can get one?"

"No. I don't think we can get one, Modge."

"What about one of them worms then?"

CHAPTER 6

I stick my nice metal key in the nice wooden door and turn it, grateful for the normality of it all. I trudge into the house, wondering if agreeing to all this is going to be the worst mistake of my life. I mean, I still don't even know what a dimension actually IS.

I'm so distracted that I don't notice the pile of suitcases in the hall till I fall over them. While I'm lying on the floor, a delicious waft of curry spices and frying poppadoms hits me and my stomach growls.

"Hello?" I shout. "Who's there?" I already know it's not my mum cooking because shepherd's pie is about her limit and even that's a bit ropey, to be honest.

"Dinner's ready!" Aunt Rekha's voice calls from the kitchen and when I get up and peer inside the whole table is heaving under the weight of all the food and my dad's sitting behind it with a napkin tucked under his chin to catch the drool.

"Ah, there you are, Danny. Come and sit down," Aunt Rekha says, adding a steaming dish of pilau rice to the table.

"What's going on?" I ask Dad, ignoring my stomach's famished grumbling. "Where's Mum?"

"Your mum's going to be staying with an old friend so she can be near the hospital," says Dad. "And Rekha kindly said she'd come and look after us."

"Oh." My throat feels all weird and tight. I know mum's got to be with grandad, but I can't believe she just left without even saying goodbye.

Aunt Rekha pats my dad's face. "Well, I can't let my baby brother starve now, can I?"

Dad looks at me. One of his "just sit down and don't cause trouble" looks.

"Won't it be nice having them here?" he says.

"I s'pose."

It doesn't feel nice though. It feels all wrong, but what can I do? I'm just a kid so no one asks me what I want. I sit down and start helping myself. Maybe food will fill the ginormous hole left behind by my grandad

AND my mum both being gone.

Aunt Rekha beams at me.

"Growing boys need their food," she says, adding three poppadoms to my already overflowing plate.

I guess it might not be so bad if she stays, I decide, stuffing a whole bhaji into my mouth.

But right then Inaaya hurries into the kitchen wearing a fluffy purple onesie and sits down opposite me. I drop my fork with a clang.

"All unpacked?" Aunt Rekha asks her.

"Yes Mum. I've unpacked and made the bed and got started on my homework," Inaaya says like some perfect evil robot child.

"SHE'S not staying here too, is she?" I demand of Dad because REPLACING my grandad AND my mum with an evil robot like Inaaya feels like some terrible cosmic prank.

"Danny! Don't be so rude!" Dad snaps.

"But Dad!"

"Of course Inaaya is staying, Aunt Rekha can't leave her behind, can she?"

"But why can't she just stay at home with Uncle Manesh and Cousin Ashwin?" I ask.

"Because they've gone to stay in Birmingham," Aunt Rekha says with a catch in her voice, looking like she's going to cry any minute.

"This is delicious, Rekha! Just like Ma used to make!" Dad says, shovelling food into his mouth in a blatant attempt at distraction.

Aunt Rekha beams at him so I guess it must work. "You're looking too thin, Rajesh, both of you are, but I'll soon have you fattened up."

I carry on eating but it's not the same. Nothing is and I don't like it.

I want Mum back. I want Grandad home.

And I definitely, absolutely, want evil robot Inaaya to explode painfully in a ball of lava fire.

I'm watching the usual rubbish after school t.v in the living room while I wait for Modge to come round and so far Inaaya has tutted at me thirty-seven times. Obviously, I have no choice but to turn the volume up each time to drown it out.

"Can you stop watching that rubbish please? I'm trying to do my homework!"

Inaaya tells me. As if it's not obvious with all the papers and books strewn all over the place and the endless scratching of her stupid pen.

"Chill out, Inaaya!" I say. "School's over. You're supposed to relax and have fun."

Inaaya glares at me. "I don't have time for fun! My astronomy project needs to be in next week and I can't concentrate with that on."

I shrug "Well, tough. This is where we watch TV. Go and do your homework in your bedroom instead."

"Ha! That's not a bedroom, it's a shoe box! There's barely enough room to sleep in there."

This is kind of true but still, she's got a cheek moaning about our house.

"If it's not good enough for you, Princess Inaaya, why don't you go home to your enormous boring old palace? No one asked you to come and stay here."

Inaaya throws her pen on the floor, makes some weird sobbing noise and runs out of the room just as the doorbell goes. Honestly, I don't know what she's got to cry about. I'm the one who's got to put up with her!

"All right?" Modge says a minute later, flopping on the sofa next to me. "Your aunt let me in. I didn't know she was staying."

"Yeah, she's staying here with Inaaya while my mum's at the hospital with Grandad."

"How long will your mum be away?"

"Dunno. Not long I hope. She annoys me like mad when she's here but when she isn't I kind of miss her, do you know what I mean?"

"Yeah . . ." Modge wipes his nose on his sleeve and stares at his trainers for ages.

"Earth to Modgeasaurus!" I say, cupping my mouth with my hand to make my voice go funny. "Come in, Modgeasaurus!"

"You're coming in loud and clear, Dannotron!" he says, perking up immediately and flashing me a massive grin. He looks just like he did when we were five and played 'Dinosaurs vs Robots' on the first day of nursery and decided we'd be best friends forever.

"Come on then, Dino Brain, we've got loads to do!" I give his shoulder a quick squeeze and jump off the sofa.

Modge practically bounces as he follows me into the hall.

I slip my trainers on and open the front door as quietly as I can, but Aunt Rekha has the same ridiculously sharp hearing as my mum and she pokes her head round the kitchen doorway and insists I comb my hair and promise to be home in time for dinner before she lets me leave.

"Ugh. They're both driving me crazy already!" I tell Modge as we hurry round to the workshop. "My aunt does nothing but clean and cook and Inaaya's been doing homework ever since she got home from school. Can you believe it? Apparently she's now an expert in astronomy or something."

"My mum's an expert in astronomy," Modge says. "She says being a Pisces is why she's so sensitive and my dad's boring because he's a Taurus."

"That's not astRONoMY, Modge, that's astROLoGY."

"Oh. What's the difference?"

I shrug. "I think astrology is star signs and astronomy is about planets and all that?"

"Is that even a subject at school?"

"Not at our school," I say. "But Inaaya goes to some posh school where everyone is called Clementine ."

Modge snorts. "What? Even the boys?"

"Probably."

We're still snorting and calling each other names like Banana and Kumquat when we reach the workshop. Then I see the sign Dad must have come round and put up on the office door this morning.

WORKSHOP CLOSED DUE TO ILL HEALTH
PLEASE PHONE THE COUNCIL FOR
ANY REPAIRS NEEDED

Someone's written underneath the sign in felt-tip pen, "Get well soon, Dougie! We miss you!" and I have to swallow down a big hard lump in my throat. Grandad's been working on this estate for twenty years and everyone knows him, everyone knows they can depend on him, and it's all MY fault he's not here to help them any more.

It's MY fault he's stuck in hospital. It's MY fault Mum's gone away. I've managed to mess everything up and I don't know how to fix it. Grandad was the one who fixed things, not me.

"Danny? Come on!" Modge says, dragging at my arm.

"Yeah, coming."

I shake the guilt away and follow him into the office and through to the workshop. As we climb into the locker, my grandad's watch tingles in my pocket and it feels like maybe he is here, a little bit at least.

The blue light swallows us up and then we're back in the IDLPO. It doesn't even seem that weird any more, which is probably because my brain is being slowly poisoned by radiation from that bright blue light.

I unlock the door with the watch/key and grab the instruction book Mrs Arburknuckle gave me. I can't quite believe I'm planning to spend my free time reading a book after a full day at school, especially a big fat boring one, but I can't let Grandad down. Not again. He asked me to look after things and I'm guessing that means looking after all this weird lost property, so that's what I'm going to do.

Anyway, old Squid-face will be back to check on us soon and I don't fancy explaining to her why we haven't done anything.

CHAPTER 7

Over an hour later and I'm still on the first page. I've finally managed to get it to translate to English by choosing it out of the hundreds of languages listed on sparkling silver pages right at the front, (including Gobbledegook, Yabba Squish Bang and Cyberdeathpunk) but I still can't understand any of it.

"Have you worked it out yet?" Modge asks for the twentieth time.

"No! I haven't even got past the introduction. None of it makes any sense!" I slam the book shut and get up to stretch my legs.

"But Danny, we better hurry up!"

"I'm trying, aren't I? It's not my fault it's written in space-nerd language."

"Yeah, but look!"

I follow Modge over to the sliding door and stare in horror at the blue net. It's bulging at the seams with all sorts of crazy stuff. I can see giant brown furry pants, an umbrella that looks like it's made from butterfly wings and bird bones, a tiny glass pot full of something golden that glows and sparkles, and there's even a set of false teeth that would fit inside a dinosaur's mouth!

"Flaming hedgehogs! What happens if it bursts?" I ask Modge, trying not to panic.

"I dunno, but I bet we'd be in trouble with Mrs Squid!"

"We have to figure out what to do, fast! Why don't you try reading the book, Modge?"

Modge makes a disgusted face.

"Or," he says, "I could try pulling that lever?"

"What lever?"

"That one!" He points behind us where a big red lever is attached to the wall.

"Wait, Modge. We don't know what it does!" I say as he sidles over to it.

"There's only one way to find out." He reaches up.

"Modge, no!" I shout but it's too late. He yanks the lever and everything in the net disappears through a hole in the floor.

"Oops," Modge says.

There's only one thing for it. It's desperate and drastic and I'm probably going to regret this forever but . . .

"Inaaya!" I whisper as loud as I can, tapping on my living-room window from outside in the back garden, where I'm hiding.

Inaaya looks up from her homework and makes a face at me. There's a teeny tiny possibility she's still annoyed with me about before. I beckon her closer. Eventually, after an AGE, she gets up and opens the back door.

"What are you doing?" she says. "Why don't you come round the front?"

"Because I don't want your mum to see me, that's why."

"Well, what do you want?"

"You."

"What?"

I sigh. "Look, Inaaya, I know we don't get on, because you're really annoying basically, but I need you to do me a big favour."

Inaaya crosses her arms. "I'm busy, Danny. I don't have time for your stupid games. Some of us have more important things to do."

"Homework?" I guess. "Homework isn't important. Not compared to this."

"You would say that. You've got no ambition. I'm going to be an astrophysicist one day."

"I do so have ambition!" I tell her. "Just because I live on a council estate doesn't mean I don't want to do stuff with my life, you know!"

"Well, maybe you should work a bit harder at school then and stop getting into trouble, or you'll end up wasting your life!"

I hate the fact that she's right. I want to tell her to shut her stupid face, but I really need her help so I just bluff it out.

"What do I need to work for?" I ask. "I'm going to be an explorer or a movie star or something else awesome that requires talent and charm which I already totally have."

"I'm sure you don't need me then. Talent and charm can fix everything," she snaps and starts to shut the door. I jam my foot in the door in a panic.

"No, wait . . . Inaaya, look, it's not for me, it's for my grandad. Pleeeease. You're the only one who can help." I make my eyes as wide as possible and blink my eyelashes until any resistance is impossible.

Inaaya shakes her head. "Really?"

"Swear." I take a deep breath. "He left me something to do, something important, just before the ambulance came. It's in his workshop and I promised him I'd do it but I can't. It's all gone wrong and I need your help. Please, Inaaya, I don't want to let him down." And I don't want my brains to leak out of my ears, so I really hope that's enough to convince her.

"Oh, all right," she says after a minute. "But only

because your grandad was always super nice to me."

"Great!" He's nice to everyone, my grandad. It's one of his major failings. But looks like it worked out this time.

"I need to tell Mum something first though."

"Say you're going to the library!"

My cousin looks horrified. "You want me to lie to my mum?"

"Inaaya, parents should never be told the truth if you can possibly help it. They can't handle it."

She makes a face, disappears for a minute and then joins me in the garden. I shut the door behind her and lead her over the fence and back round to the workshop where I left Modge with strict instructions not to touch anything.

"What's this thing you promised to do then?" Inaaya asks.

"I can't tell you,"

"Why not?"

"Because."

"Because what?"

"Because . . . I kind of promised I wouldn't tell anyone."

"Then how am I supposed to help?"

"It's all right," I reassure her. "I can't tell you, but I'm pretty sure I can show you." At least, I hope I can.

It's not exactly easy to shove Inaaya into the locker but I manage it eventually and when I squish in behind her my grandad's watch tingles, the blue light flashes and we fall out into the waiting room.

"WHY DID YOU PUSH ME IN HERE, YOU MASSIVE BANANA-BRAINED IDIOT?" Inaaya yells at me as she stumbles to her feet.

"I had to!" I protest. "I couldn't tell you what I was doing, I signed a contract to keep it a secret."

"Keep what a secret? That you like shoving girls into lockers?"

"We're not in the locker now though, are we?" I spread one arm out wide like a magician revealing an amazing trick.

Inaaya opens and then shuts her mouth like a startled fish. Her eyes widen. "What's going on? Where are we? You better tell me right now or I'm going to thump you!"

I hold my hands up. "All right, She-Ra. No need to get violent. If you come with me, I can show you."

I head over to the office door and open it with the watch. Inaaya grits her teeth but she's too curious not to follow.

"Danny!" Modge shouts when he sees me. "Did you bring any biscuits?"

"I didn't go to get biscuits. I went to get help."

"Yeah, but biscuits help everything," Modge points out.

"Yeah, well, Inaaya will help more."

"Are you sure?" Modge asks, looking doubtfully at Inaaya.

"Inaaya will smack both your heads together if you don't shut up about biscuits and tell me what's going on!" Inaaya growls.

Modge makes a face at me. "Not taking it very well, is she?"

To save Modge from getting thumped, I grab the log book off the desk and shove it in front of Inaaya's face.

"The Interdimensional Lost Property Office Official Log Book," she reads out loud. Then frowns. Then reads it again. Then she opens the book and her mouth drops open. "Are you trying to tell me this is an interdimensional lost property office?" she says at last. "A REAL one?"

I stare at her. "What do you mean, a real one?"

Her eyes light up as she talks and her hands wave around in the air. "Well, there were a few rumours, on these space chatrooms I sometimes use, that they might exist. In a multiversal reality there would always be some crossing over, weak points, worm holes etcetera. And things are always going missing, aren't

they? And they're never found again! Where do they all go?"

I've never seen her so excited.

"So you actually know what an interdimensional multiverse is then?" I ask.

"There are a couple of hypotheses, but my favourite one is that dimensions are stacked on top of each other like plates . . ."

"That makes sense because of the big pillar thing Mrs Arburknuckle told us about, doesn't it Danny?"

Inaaya doesn't hear him but I nod at Modge because he's right. That big pillar thing holding up all of these plate dimensions does make a weird kind of sense, especially if you ignore the fact that NONE of this makes any sense.

"And although the dimensions are essentially the same, each one will have some sort of difference that affects everything within that dimension," Inaaya continues breathlessly.

"So you're saying there are loads of worlds just like this one but different?" I ask.

Modge's ears prick up. "Does that mean there are loads of Modges?"

"Possibly," says Inaaya. "Every single choice within each dimension can create massive change, so you probably exist in some but not in others."

My head is spinning at all the possibilities, but I try and focus on the most important thing – which is getting Inaaya's help to fix things.

"Right, well, this place was my grandad's," I say. "He's been working here for years and now he's left me in charge while he's in hospital."

"I can't believe there's an interdimensional lost property office HERE!" Inaaya practically squeals. "On a scummy old council estate!"

"Oy! It's not scummy!"

"All right, but it's still crazy! Why is it here of all places?"

"Because of the wyrm eating a hole in the pillar," Modge says.

Inaaya opens her mouth to argue, thinks better of it and looks at me instead. "And your grandad's been running it for years and he never said anything to you?"

"I just thought he was the caretaker of our estate," I admit. "I only found out he was caretaker of the

IDLPO yesterday when we accidentally came through the locker."

"You are SO lucky, Danny!"

I'm not sure lucky is the word I'd use but I decide it's best not to argue.

"Yeah," I say instead. "Only we don't know what to do and I can't understand the instruction manual Mrs Arburknuckle left and then Modge pulled a lever and . . ." I swallow.

"What?"

"We lost it," I admit.

"Lost what?"

"The lost property. We lost the lost property."

"You lost the lost property?" Inaaya repeats.

"Yes."

"How?"

"I'll show you."

I hurry over to the sliding door and pull it back.

CHAPTER 8

Inaaya wanders in slowly and stares in awe at the empty sparkly net. "That lost property is actual evidence of the existence of other dimensions, you know! Or it would be if you two idiots hadn't managed to lose it all!" she sighs.

"It's not our fault," I protest. "That blue net thing was really full and we thought it might burst, so Modge pulled this lever on the wall and everything in it fell down a hole in the floor."

Inaaya sighs again, even louder. "Where's this instruction manual you keep talking about?"

"Here." Modge gives her the book and Inaaya flicks through it quickly.

"Aha! There's a basic guide here."

"Is there?" I peer over her shoulder but all I can see are some weird pointy diagrams and endless writing next to it.

"It's quite straightforward really," says Inaaya. "Pulling the lever is the first stage, but then you have to press the button on top to activate the whadjamacallit."

Modge snorts. "The whadjamacallit?"

"That's what the sorting machine is called!"

I look at the lever and see a fat round button on top, just as Inaaya said. I press it with my thumb.

There's a gentle hum in the room before a shiny, rainbow-coloured machine rises right up from the floor along the far edges of the room. There's a long silver ribbon that moves like a conveyor belt and further along it flows through a large blue metal box and out the other side. It reminds me a bit of the X-Ray machine I saw at the airport last year, so they can look inside your luggage.

Next to the box there's a big flat screen that lights up as the items rise up from wherever they've been and begin to move gently along the silver belt towards the box.

"That's a scanner," Inaaya says, pointing at the blue box. "It will fully analyse the item so it can be properly labelled and stored until its owner files a report."

"Ha! I knew you'd be fluent in space nerd!" I slap her on the shoulder, the relief making me a bit giddy.

"You're a genius!" Modge says.

"Not really," Inaaya says, trying to sound modest but failing. "I just can't believe I'm here. In a real interdimensional lost property office. And look, there's the first item coming up now!"

We all watch with bated breath as something that looks like a large lump of grey rock disappears into the blue box.

"There could be an entire universe inside that rock!" Inaaya says.

"Or, maybe it's an alien egg!" Modge suggests.

"No! I bet it's a mini spaceship!"

The screen flickers and we all stare at it fixedly until words appear.

```
Item Scan Complete
Dimension Urgle Bor 56
Item 3677777821b* ——— A Rock
```

Disappointment fills the room.

"Okay, but it is still a rock from another dimension!" Inaaya says, like that helps.

The rock emerges from the scanner and keeps moving along the conveyor belt. A small cardboard box is already waiting at the other end for the rock to fall in to.

Inaaya looks at the manual again. "Each item scan produces the perfect storage solution from the packager. All we have to do is tape up the box and stick the label on."

Modge grabs the dispenser and runs the purple tape with IDLPO printed on it in shiny silver letters over the box edges. I grab the printed label as it comes out and stick it on the box.

The box keeps trundling along the silver belt and then falls through a flap and disappears.

"That will take it down to the store room, where it stays till someone claims it," Inaaya says, reading from the book.

"We did it," Modge says. "Our first item."

I feel a strange sense of satisfaction. We did do it. Though I'm not sure who's going to be missing a rock.

"Ooh, here comes the next item!" Modge shouts, and we all turn and stare, trying not to get our hopes up.

"Is that a pencil?" I ask.

"Please be something more than a pencil," Modge begs.

```
Item scan complete
Dimension 7Vx22
Item 3769871248d* ——— A Pencil . . .
```

We all groan.

```
. . . -Laser-Blaster-Matter-Dematerialiser
```

We all cheer.

"Wow! That is SO cool!" Modge says, beaming. "What does it do?"

"If you shoot it at something, the laser will make it disappear," Inaaya explains.

Modge's eyes expand and his hand reaches for the pencil as it falls into the box.

"NO!" Inaaya shouts, grabbing Modge's arm and yanking it away from the pencil. "We're not allowed to touch anything! It's too dangerous and we definitely can't ever take anything out of here. Using something from another dimension in our dimension could cause an interdimensional cross anomaly."

"A what now?" I say.

Inaaya rolls her eyes. "Umm, like a small explosion that rips everything apart and causes the entire dimensional infrastructure to disintegrate."

"Well, that's rubbish!" Modge says. "All this brilliant stuff and we can't touch any of it or take anything out into our world? What's the point of that?"

"It's not a toyshop, Modge," Inaaya says, with a sniff. "We are the guardians of an interdimensional treasure chest. If these items got into the wrong hands it could be devastating to the entire structure of interdimensionality!"

"Yeah, but we should get SOME cool stuff!" Modge says with a huff.

I'm not so sure though. All this cool stuff is starting to look WAY more dangerous.

"You just said WE are the guardians, Inaaya," I say.

"And?"

"Does that mean you want to stay and help?" As much as I hate to admit it, I think we definitely need her if this is going to work. I can't let Grandad down just because Inaaya is annoying.

"Oh, you have to let me stay and be a part of this, Danny!" Inaaya pleads. "You will, won't you? I can make a study of it and write a paper. I'll be famous. Universities will be begging me to study there!"

"Inaaya, you can't tell anyone about this," I warn. "Not ever. You'll have to sign a contract and everything."

"Yeah, and if you do tell your brain will turn to MUSH!" Modge informs her with bloodthirsty glee.

Inaaya deflates a little but then nods. "I still want to stay and help, Danny. I can't miss this experience."

"Okay then," I say. "The three of us will look after everything until my grandad's better," "Agreed?"

Modge and Inaaya both nod but I insist on a fist

bump each to seal the deal and decide to wait till
Mrs A is in a good mood before I explain it all to her.

Two hours into clearing the backlog and it's all a bit of
a mess. Modge has bits of sticky pink goop dripping
from his hair, after accidentally poking an exploding
'snurble-pod,' and I'm nursing a painful bite on my
finger from a tiny grumpy leather purse that fell off
the conveyor belt and attacked me.

Inaaya went on and on about how it was all our
own fault for touching things we weren't supposed to,
but then she flung her plait over her shoulder and the
end got caught on a spiky wickenflugger crystal which
burst into green flames and she finally had to shut up
and concentrate on putting her hair out instead.

I have no idea how my grandad managed to do this
job for years. It's EXHAUSTING. Even the really good stuff
– like the huge, shiny jewelled sword, the fairy wand
with wings, the humungous pair of furry troll pants,
or the jar of invisibility powder – isn't that exciting
because we can't touch ANY of it, so it's like being out

of pocket money in the best toy shop in the world.

Also, none of our phones work in here – Inaaya says it's something to do with the signal being affected by the wyrm hole – so there's nothing else to do but work.

"Can we stop now?" Modge says, slapping another label on the box. "I'm starving."

"That was the last item, so I guess so," I tell him.

"I'll turn off the whadjamacallit then," Inaaya says in her bossiest voice.

She presses the button on the lever and the machine turns off and slowly sinks back in to the floor.

We leave the back room with the blue net gently glowing, waiting for any new lost property to arrive – just as the office door bursts open and Mrs Arburnuckle ploughs through on her Segway.

"Who is that?" she demands, glaring at Inaaya, who's actually speechless for once in her life. "And what is she doing here? Did you not listen when I said this was top secret? Surely your brains should have melted . . ." She peers at me and Modge, looking for signs of leaking brains.

"I didn't tell her anything," I explain. "I just showed

her instead."

Mrs Arburknuckle makes a noise like a grumpy gibbon. "Younglings from this dimension seem to be exceptionally sneaky! There will be no more SHOWING anyone, do you understand?"

"I do, honest," I say. "But we needed Inaaya's help cos she can read space nerd. And we've got everything working now and the backlog is all sorted, so you should be happy really."

"Wow," Inaaya finally says, goggling at Mrs Arburknuckle like she's some new science experiment.

"Er, Inaaya, this is our supervisor Mrs Arburknuckle," I say.

Mrs Arburknuckle gets out her silver pad and insists Inaaya signs the secrecy order immediately.

"I hope you can keep secrets, young lady or you may find your brains leaking out of your ears!"

"Oh, I can, don't worry about that! You can tell me anything. Like what dimension you come from and how you travel between them and how you can speak our language so well," Inaaya says, pressing her hand on the screen and yelping.

Mrs Arburknuckle ignores her entirely. "That

reminds me, I have located some widgets for you. They'll enable you to understand and speak most of the languages you might come across in your work, whether spoken or written."

"Oh wow! That sounds amazing!" Inaaya says, pain forgotten.

Mrs A opens a small box. Inside are a dozen wriggling white grubs about the length of my little finger. They look a bit like woodlice with long feelers on the front and loads of tiny, tiny legs underneath and are so NOT what I was expecting.

"Take one widget each," she says and we reluctantly follow her command.

"Urgh!" Modge says, holding his at arm's length. "What are they for?"

"They're going to help us understand other languages, Modge, from other dimensions," Inaaya tells him, gazing lovingly at her wriggly widget grub. "Do you know how lucky we are?"

"Now just stick them up a nostril," Mrs Arburknuckle instructs us.

"WHAT?" Inaaya demands, not looking quite so thrilled any more.

"Come on now, you won't feel a thing."

"Yeah, come on then, Inaaya. You first. Show us how lucky we are!" Modge tells her.

Inaaya gulps hard and then moves the grub near her nose. Me and Modge watch in disgusted amazement as the grub wriggles up her nostril and disappears inside.

"Argh! I can feel it moving!" Inaaya shouts, dancing up and down,

"Of course it's moving, dear, it needs to reach your brain . . ."

"WHAAT!" Inaaya yelps like she's just trod on a Lego piece.

"Once it's linked into your language core you won't even notice it."

A minute or so passes and then Inaaya's face clears and she smiles. "It's okay. It's fine."

There's no other choice now. If Inaaya's done it, then we have to do it too or she'll never stop lording it over us.

It's not EXACTLY fun but it's not that bad, a bit like taking horrible medicine while your mum pinches your nose shut to make you swallow.

"A quick test then!" Mrs Arburknuckle announces, pulling a newspaper out of her Segway basket. "The latest IDLPO newsletter from Centralus. It's written in Qwerty – the official language of Centralus, but you should be able to read it now."

She holds it out so I can see, but the letters on the front page look like some weird sort of hieroglyphics.

$'\{\bullet-\sqrt{}+\times \geq \{\emptyset \geq^-]\sqrt{}\{+\geq [>\propto \approx\}\{\sqrt{}- \sqrt{\bullet}^-$
$-\propto \geq^- \geq > -]\sqrt{}+\sqrt{} >\Delta\Sigma\mu =\Omega\mu-]\mu<<\leqslant"$

But when I blink the headline suddenly reads like English. The widgets are working!

"CENTRALUS HUB EXPERIMENT SOON TO BE EXTENDED!" I read out loud. "Billionaire benefactors thrilled with success and . . ."

"My turn!" Inaaya shouts, snatching the paper out of Mrs Arburknuckles tentacle and immediately reading it.

"Sorry about her," I mutter.

"No need to apologise for enthusiasm. I'll just finish my inspection and leave you to it."

She zooms off into the sorting room and emerges a few minutes later.

"I'm very glad to see that backlog is gone Danny, well done," Mrs Arburknuckle says.

"Told you we could do it!" Modge says.

"Carry on the good work then but remember, NO MORE additions to the team!" Mrs Arburknuckle says, with a quick glance at Inaaya sitting cross-legged on the floor reading the newsletter.

"There definitely won't be," I promise. "Inaaya is more than enough."

Mrs Arburknuckle gives a rare chuckle before disappearing and it starts to sink in that I'm going to be stuck with my cousin at home AND at the IDLPO.

"Cheer up, Danny!" Modge says, clapping me on the shoulder. "Maybe your grandad will make a quick recovery?"

"I hope so Modge," I mutter, "or I might have to accidentally use that laser-blaster pencil."

Modge grins at me but I'm not even joking.

CHAPTER 9

The next afternoon after school me and Modge half-heartedly help Inaaya sort out the day's lost property, but when she's not looking we sneak off to the front office where we can eat biscuits and pretend to write up the log book.

"Three-eyed fish are SO cool!" Modge says, dancing around the fish tank like an overexcited toddler. He loves animals but his dad has so many allergies he's not allowed any pets. Not even a fish.

I toss a Jammy Dodger in the air and manage to catch it in my mouth while twirling around in the big chair. "Yes!" I pump the air with my fist.

Modge stands still. "My turn, Danny!"

I lob one in his direction but he misses and it lands in the fish tank instead. A tiny fish mouth shoots out of the big fish mouth, snatches the biscuit and disappears back inside.

"WHOA!" I yell. "Now THAT was cool!"

"Imagine if we could take him into school!" Modge says, jumping up and down. "We'd be in the papers and everything. We'd be famous!"

"Yeah, but we can't."

"It's not fair though, Danny! Nothing is fair!" Modge practically shouts, which seems a teeny bit of an overreaction.

"What do you mean?" I ask him. "What isn't fair?"

Modge looks on the brink of telling me something important but sighs and turns away instead.

"Modge? What is it?" I ask again, hoping he'll finally tell me what's been bothering him the last few days – but the plant lights growing across the ceiling start flashing red and a loud alarm sounds.

Modge and me run into the back room where Inaaya is calmly taping up boxes.

"What's going on? What did you do?" I demand. I'm panicking a tiny bit because I can't have anything going wrong.

"I didn't do anything," Inaaya protests. "The machine just started going haywire."

"Ooh! Looook!" Modge breathes, his finger pointing at the conveyor belt where a round glass ball is moving towards us. It's not the ball that's got him excited, though. It's the creature trapped inside.

I've never seen anything like it.

It's about the size of a kitten and covered in black metallic fur. It has a long, segmented tail that whips back and forth, and two legs, one on either side that whirl round in circles as it tries to escape.

Modge is practically vibrating with excitement. "What is it? What is it?"

A second later it hits the scanner and a read out comes up.

```
Squiddleflex Primo from Dimension
7Vx22
Rare
Interdimensional transport to
Centralus Hub activated
```

"Wow! A Squiddleflex Primo!" Modge says like he knows exactly what that is. "Let's keep it here for a while and see what it does –"

But it's too late. Inaaya has already pulled the label off the printer and as soon as she sticks it to the globe a big blue spiral of light descends from the ceiling.

"WARNING! HUB TRANSPORTATION COMMENCING! CLEAR AREA!" the scanner repeats over and over.

And with a sudden whoosh the Squiddleflex in its glass prison is sucked upwards and disappears. The blue spiral is gone a second later and all that's left is the sound of Modge wailing.

"Why did you do that?" he demands of Inaaya.

"That's what I'm supposed to do!" says Inaaya. "The new trial means all living creatures get sent to the hub where they're processed and then returned to their own dimensions."

"So? You don't always have to do everything you're supposed to do!"

Inaaya frowns. "What were you going to do with that thing anyway? You can't just keep random creatures as pets."

Modge thrusts his bottom lip out. "Don't tell me what to do! I'm fed up with people telling me what to do all the time!"

"Danny, you tell him!"

I stare at the pair of them facing off like two dogs in a fight and hold my hands up. "Let's just all calm down."

"It's best for it to go to the Hub!" Inaaya insists. "You don't know anything about that creature, Modge. Not what it eats or how to look after it or anything!"

Modge's jaw clenches. "Well, how do YOU know that THEY look after the creatures properly at the stupid Hub?"

Inaaya sighs. "Because it's a huge brand-new purpose-built facility, Modge! It's been specially designed and everything. There's a big feature about it in the newsletter, see?" She pulls it out of her bag, pointing at the picture of a huge glass and chrome space station, shaped like a circle with a big cross running through the middle. "Every creature who gets sent there has a full medical and any treatment they need, and then they can go right back to their homes as soon as possible."

Modge peers at the newsletter. In the lower corner – under the words "Amazingly generous donation from Kaspar and Kaylar Arachnus from the Dimension Zonama!" – there's a small picture of two glossy, smiling, surprisingly human-like people. "Well, they can say anything they like in the paper, can't they?" he says in his sulky voice. "Doesn't mean it's true."

Inaaya makes a noise like a wounded seal. "Why would they lie? That doesn't even make sense."

"Papers lie all the time, Inaaya! You can't trust them. Everyone knows that."

"All right, enough," I say before another fight breaks out. "It's gone now and we can't change it, so let's just forget it and get back to work."

Modge glares at me then stomps off to stare at the fish again. Inaaya glares at me like this is all my fault and then goes back to sorting the rest of the lost property as loudly as she can.

If this is what I get for being the sensible one, I'm not sure it's all it's cracked up to be.

"Danny? Can you tell your friend to stop humming?"

"Danny? Can you tell your cousin to get stuffed?"

"Danny? Tell your little friend to go jump in the lake, will you?"

"Danny? Tell ANNOYA to shut her ANNOYing face."

"Danny? Tell SPLODGE . . ."

I have to walk into the front office and shut the door behind me before I thump them both. They've been sniping at each other ever since their argument yesterday, and playing piggy in the middle is driving me MAD.

Five minutes of peace is all I want but three minutes and fifty-two seconds is all I actually get because the stupid poxy alarm goes off again. By the time I slide the back door open Modge and Inaaya are practically wrestling over the glass ball in the scanner.

"What are you doing? STOP IT!" I yell.

The alarm stops clanging on my command which is pleasing, but Inaaya and Modge just carry on with their nonsense like I'm not even there.

"Tell him to let go!" Inaaya shouts.

"Why should I?" Modge demands.

"Because it's the rules! If we don't follow them, we'll get into trouble!"

"It's not up to you, bossy pants!"

"Just let go, you big stupid head!"

I've decided I've had enough and march over to drag them both apart, but Inaaya manages to stretch far enough to grab the label and slaps it on to the orb.

The blue spiral descends.

"WARNING! HUB TRANSPORTATION COMMENCING! CLEAR AREA!"

"Let go! Now!" I yell but neither of them listen. I grab hold of Modge's foot and Inaaya's arm to try and drag them away but it's too late.

The powerful
suction from the
spiral drags the orb inside,
with Inaaya and Modge still
stubbornly clinging to it.
Obviously this means that I'M
pulled up into the swirling vortex of doom
– right alongside them.

Once, when me and Modge were younger, we took a big old plastic bin up to the top of Purley Hill, climbed inside and rolled all the way down for a laugh.

We both ended up in Casualty with broken fingers and sprained wrists and about a million bruises and scratches. Mum said it was the most stupid thing we'd ever done. But it's got NOTHING on being sucked up inside a vortex of time and space and being spat out in some random dimension with no way to get back home again.

I don't even know who I am for a long minute and when I DO remember I almost wish I hadn't.

Reluctantly I open my eyes but everything's spinning like that time I went on the waltzer at the fair three times in a row. I close them again and try really hard not to panic.

On one side I can hear someone retching.

On the other someone is groaning.

I'd enjoy the sounds of their suffering more if I wasn't quite so miserable myself.

"Danny?" Modge's voice is croaky and frail but I have no sympathy. "Are you alive?"

"No thanks to you two," I whisper.

"It was his fault!"

"It was her fault!"

"Shut up!" I shout and they fall silent. "You're both idiots and now look what's happened!"

The burst of anger gives me the energy to open my eyes again and try sitting up. My stomach rebels but I swallow hard and manage to keep my lunch down.

As far as I can tell we're in some sort of dimly lit box, which doesn't exactly fill me with confidence.

"We must be at the Hub," Inaaya says, a trace of excitement leaking through the grogginess.

"Ooh, well done, Sherlock!" I snap. "Now can you please tell me how we get home again!"

"At least Shugly's all right," Modge says.

"Who?"

"Shugly! That's what I'm calling him." Modge holds up a small fuzzy round creature with six small legs, two big eyes that pop out from its head on stalks and a tiny little silver horn in between.

"What is it?" I ask, unable to stop myself stroking its soft fuzz with one finger.

"A Fligglenog!" says Modge like a proud father. "That's what the scanner said. Isn't he cool?"

"Did you take it out of the globe?" Inaaya demands.

"No! The globe just opened when we got here," Mogde says, snuggling the creature close to his chest like a weird squishy baby.

"Well, don't get too attached," Inaaya warns. "We're leaving that thing here when we go."

Modge pokes his tongue out at Inaaya just as the floor drops away beneath our feet and we land in a plastic wagon that whizzes rapidly along a thick track. A curved see-through lid is placed on top of us by robotic arms and swiftly seals around the edges, keeping us trapped inside.

Hundreds more wagons are on the same track, which snakes around a humungous warehouse. Every single wagon is filled with ridiculous creatures. The three of us gawk through our glass lid at the variety of weird heads and paws and claws and eyes and tails zooming around.

"Wow! This is an amazing place!" Inaaya says. "There must be hundreds of creatures here."

"Yeah, but we're not creatures! How do we get out

of this thing?" I poke at the glass lid to see if it will
shift but it's firmly stuck down.

"Where do you think they're taking us?" Modge asks.

"I suppose we'll get scanned and then they'll
realise we don't belong here and come and get us
out," Inaaya says, like it's all perfectly reasonable.

"How are we going to explain this?" I ask her.

She shrugs. "We'll just say we made a mistake and
they'll send us home."

"And what if they tell Mrs Arburknuckle what
happened?" I demand. "What if she decides we're
not responsible enough to run the IDLPO anymore? I
promised my grandad I was going to look after things
and you two were supposed to be helping me, not
getting me into trouble!"

"We didn't mean it," Modge mutters.

"I know! I know you didn't mean it, but I just
wanted to get things right for once!" I explode. "Prove
to Grandad I can be responsible and now it's all
messed up!"

We sit there in silence as the cart speeds along the
track. All I can think about is the disappointment on
Grandad's face when I tell him I messed up. Again.

CHAPTER 10

"Come on," Inaaya says after a minute. "Help me!"

"What?"

"With the roof!" She starts trying to pry the edge of the glass lid loose from our cart. "I'm getting us out of here, so just help me!"

Me and Modge pull and tug at the seal but it's stuck fast.

"Here!" Inaaya calls, finding a loose bit, and the three of us help her tear it away. The rest of it comes easily and we shove the lid off and let it tumble down to the floor way below.

"Now what?" I ask her as the breeze from our speed whips at our hair.

"We jump," she says, pointing a finger at a long metal platform coming up on our left. "There!"

"Are you mad?"

"If we don't want to get caught, we

need to get out of here before they find us, right?"
says Inaaya. "This is how we do it. We can leave that
Fligglething in here and go!"

"I'm not leaving him!" Modge insists.

"We can't keep him! We'd get into loads of
trouble."

"She's right, Modge," I tell him. "You don't know
how to look after him or anything. He's better off
here."

"We don't have time to argue! Come on!" Inaaya
says.

"Are you sure this is safe?" I ask.

"Better than going through that!" she says, jerking
her chin ahead.

A sign proclaims a 'Cleaning Area', and beyond
that the carts are being filled with some sort of
brown powder through a thin copper pipe in the
roof. Whatever it is it reeks like rotten onions.
Seconds later, a million swarming beetles are
pumped into the cart through a big silver pipe and
cover the creatures like an ever-moving coat. I can
feel my skin itching already just from watching, so
the creatures must be really suffering. There's a

green skinny dog with two tails and a row of spikes along its back in the nearest cart and it bleats and paws at the glass, its eyes bulging as the beetles rise up and over its head.

"What are they doing to them?" Modge asks in horror, clutching Shugly to his chest.

"Let's not find out," I say with a shudder.

Inaaya says. "Just leave that thing here and jump!"

She climbs up on the edge and throws herself at the platform, landing neatly like a cat.

"You go next!" I tell Modge.

"I'm not leaving Shugly to get eaten by bugs!" Modge says.

"Fine! Just go!" I tell him because we don't have time to argue.

He tucks Shugly down his top and chucks himself over the edge like a cuckoo chick learning to fly and lands in a messy heap on the other side.

The cleaning station is getting closer. The smell is getting stronger. The risk of getting a stinky beetle bath threatens. I try not to think about how high up we are, or the distance I need to jump and just grit my teeth and launch myself at the platform like Indiana Jones's younger but way more handsome brother.

If my foot hadn't slipped on the rim, I might even have made it.

CHAPTER 11

Visions of my body splattered on the ground like a ripe watermelon fill my head. But as my sweaty fingers lose their grip on the edge of the platform, Inaaya and Modge reach down to grab my hands and help me scramble up on to safe ground. I lie there for a bit, panting and trying not to imagine what would have happened if I'd fallen.

"Thank you," I manage after a minute.

"We couldn't let you fall, Danny," Inaaya says and some of my anger melts away. "You're the one with the key. I don't think we can get home without it."

"Oh right," I say. "Glad to know you've got a good reason to save my life."

She grins and holds out her hand to pull me up.

Modge slaps me on the back. "You might need to practise your jumping though, mate. That was pretty lame."

"I slipped!" I tell him. "Besides, I had the furthest to jump didn't I, cos I let you two go first."

"Yeah, yeah."

"It's true!"

"I reckon Shugly could do a better jump than that," says Modge. Shugly's head emerges from his top and Modge scoops him out and gives him a cuddle. "Couldn't you, my little snugglebear? Who's a good snugglebear?"

Inaaya snorts with laughter and I join in.

"What?" Modge says.

"Snugglebear?" Inaaya says. "Really?"

I shake my head. "Mate. That's just embarrassing."

"So what's the plan now then?" Modge asks. His ears have gone a bit pink so he's obviously desperate to change the subject.

"Well, I suppose we'll have a quick look round to reassure Modge it's okay to leave 'ickle snugglebear' here and then get home as fast as we can without anyone noticing we were ever here." Inaaya says.

"And how do we do that, exactly?" I ask.

"This place is a huge, automated warehouse. We

can just follow the signs to the exit," Inaaya says. "I'm pretty sure there's no one here to even notice us. Trust me!"

She pushes open the door in the wall and we step out into the corridor. Hands clamp down on our shoulders almost immediately and we freeze in place.

"Lost, are we?" A low and sinister voice asks.

"Y . . . y . . . yes?" Inaaya says.

"I see." A shiver runs up my spine. "Well, we'll have to do something about that, won't we?"

CHAPTER 12

"You got lost on your way to the DoPS, I imagine? Everyone does." The ominous voice belongs to someone who looks almost human, except infinitely better and kind of shiny. Everything about him, from his pale skin to his fair hair, is glossy and perfect and fake, like one of those weird, filtered selfies on Instagram.

"DoPs?" I ask.

"Department of Personal Sanitation!" he tells me, by which I think he means the loo. "You'll have missed most of the tour by now, but we should be in time for the presentation."

"T . . . tour?" Inaaya stammers.

He smiles, showing a row of shiny pointy teeth. "We thought it was best if we let all of you caretakers see exactly what it is we do here at the Hub, and put your minds at rest about our future plans."

"Oh . . . yes. Of course. Excellent idea," Inaaya says, shooting relieved glances at me and Modge because it looks like we just got super lucky.

Our guide opens his arms wide, encircling us all and gently pushing us forward along the corridor.

"Hey," Modge says suddenly. "I recognise you! You're that man! From the newsletter!"

The man bows his head. "Ah, yes. I am Kaspar Arachnus, so lovely to meet you."

"You're Kaspar Arachnus?" Inaaya says, awe in her voice. "You're the billionaire who donated this entire Hub to Centralus?"

"I am."

"And YOU'RE running the tours?"

"Who better?" Kaspar asks. "My sister and I want to personally assure all of the Caretakers that our intentions here are entirely trustworthy."

"I think it's a wonderful thing you've done, donating this all to Centralus," Inaaya says and I catch Modge rolling his eyes at her sucking up. "So. How many creatures come through here every day?"

Kaspar pauses and presses a button on his wrist

and a screen flashes up on the corridor wall with
writing on it.

```
Creatures sent home today — 336
. . . 338 . . . 339 . . .
```

"We usually go up to five hundred per day," Kaspar
says.

"A DAY?" I gasp. "But how do you manage that?"
"Most of the facility is fully automated, so it's very
fast and efficient," He informs us, looking excessively
smug. "Ninety-four per cent of the creatures that
come through go straight back out again once they're
scanned. The remaining few that require our help
are sent to the only staffed area for special care, until
they're well enough to be sent home."

The screen changes.

```
Total creatures sent home — 460213
```

"Wow!" Inaaya breathes.
"That's our figure over six months with just ten
per cent of the total IDLPOs taking part," says Kaspar.

"Once Centralus signs off and we go fully online, we'll be processing up to a million creatures a year." I suppose I can see the benefits of having one big automated centre, but it's all so impersonal it makes me feel a bit sad for the creatures. That poor skinny dog on the coaster was terrified by it all.

Our guide keeps marching us along miles of sterile corridors and we have to scurry to keep up.

"Are those the pipes the beetles come through?" Modge asks, pointing at the silver pipes running along the walls. "The ones from the cleaning station?"

"Oh, you saw that, did you?" Kaspar frowns briefly. "Yes, we breed the beetles here in special nests around the Hub. The pipes run between them all and provide us with a regular supply for cleaning."

"Why do you use beetles?" Inaaya asks.

Kaspar hides a sigh behind another overly wide smile."Oh, they're just brilliant for ensuring every creature we send back is in pristine condition with no skin conditions, parasites or unsavoury hygiene issues."

"How come the beetles do what you want?" Modge demands.

I definitely hear a sigh this time before he answers.

"We cover our subjects in a special powder first that runs through the copper pipes. The beetles can't resist it. Their saliva contains an unbeatable anti-bacterial agent, and as they lick the powder off they clean the skin."

I can't help a shiver at the thought of millions of beetle tongues slobbering all over me.

"Does it hurt?" Modge looks anxious. "Does it hurt the creatures?"

"Of course not!" Kaspar insists, obvious annoyance leaking into his words now. "It's barely a tickle and over very quickly. But the thought does make some people a little queasy, so we prefer to keep this particular innovation quiet."

He smiles at us again but somehow all those shiny teeth only make me feel nervous, like being smiled at by a shark.

"Ah," he says, "I think we've caught up with the rest of the tour at their final stop, the creature rehabilitation centre!"

"That will be very interesting, won't it, Modge?" Inaaya says.

But Modge only huffs and secretly pets Shugly who's now hiding inside his pocket. I'm not sure he's going to give up his new pet, even if they're feeding them caviar and massaging their paws 24/7.

CHAPTER 13

The infirmary is just as shiny as our host, with pristine medical equipment lined up on shelves and a few glass cages with cute creatures sitting inside, with a bandaged paw or a drip running into a leg.

'This is our veterinarian, Dr Triffle Iffle," Kaspar says, waving at a short, frog-faced man with a pouffy tail that wags across the floor.

"WELCOME," the vet booms at us, bowing several times. "Here we have cutting-edge medical technology available to heal any sick creature that comes here. I dedicate my whole life to their care and wellbeing and am very grateful for job like this." He sounds like he's reading from a script or something and bows at Kaspar, wagging his tail like a puppy desperate for approval.

Kaspar smiles. "We are grateful to have such an experienced

professional working with us. As we promised when the Hub was set up, the care of lost creatures is our utmost priority. Not only can we streamline the entire process, but the creatures will receive far better care here than they would at the IDLPOs."

There's some rebellious muttering from the other caretakers milling around the infirmary. I can't help staring at them all and wondering if any of them know my grandad.

There's one chap with rippling scales all over his seal-shaped body, and another man with a giraffe neck and a tiny head with a flat cap perched on the top. One woman has hair like a wild garden with insects scurrying around in it, and a very short man has a long nose like a shrew with a whiskery moustache and ears the size of dinner plates.

"Wasn't nothing wrong with the old system if you ask me," the garden-haired woman says loudly. "This place is a huge waste of money."

"I liked looking after the creatures," pipes up another caretaker with a body made up of stones with green and purple moss growing all over her. "Made a nice change visiting the other dimensions to take them back."

A tall woman I recognise as Kaspar's sister Kaylar (mainly because she looks like his eerily perfect twin, except she has long hair and slight curves) calls out across the infirmary, "Could you all please follow me into the hall for our presentation now! Thank you so much."

We follow the other seven or so caretakers through a door and shuffle into a small hall with seats set out in front of a large screen. Me and Modge drag Inaaya away from the front row and force her to sit at the back with us like a normal person.

Kaspar and Kaylar stand at the front, looking like creepy clones of each other and smiling widely. "Please watch this short presentation and then we can take any questions at the end," Kaylar says.

A series of slides come up on the screen, with statistics and pictures and a really patronising voiceover about how beneficial the Hub will be, saving time and effort and blah blah blah.

"Isn't it lucky Mrs A gave us

those widgets?" Inaaya says, beaming. "Now we can understand the whole presentation."

I shake my head at her utter nerdery and wonder how we can possibly be related. The slide show waffles on and on, so I tune it out and take my grandad's watch out of my pocket instead. It feels a bit like he's here with me when I hold it and that eases the constant ache of missing him.

"Here, you must be Duggie's lad!" The short, shrew-faced man says under his breath, turning round to look at me.

I startle. "How do you know that?"

"That's his watch. He wouldn't have given that to anyone but his grandson."

"He talked about me?" Surprise leaks out of my voice.

"Aye, lad. He's got high hopes for you." A warm feeling spreads across my chest. "I thought he'd be here today kicking up a fuss about all this nonsense."

"Oh, he's in hospital." I tell him, wishing I knew when he was coming home, but Mum just keeps saying it will take time. "He left me in charge."

"I'm sorry to hear that lad. Tell him Murgatroyd sends his best."

I nod and smile as he turns back round. I give my grandad's watch one last gentle stroke and tuck it safely away in my pocket.

"Danny!" Modge hisses in my ear.

"What?"

"Shugly escaped from my pocket. I have to go and find him."

Modge gets on his knees and wriggles past me and back into the infirmary. I consider staying put, but who knows how many creatures Modge might come back with if I leave him alone so I follow him out.

"Where is he?" I whisper. There's no sign of the vet with the poufy tail, so that's something.

"I think he's just over there. Maybe he smelled some food or something." Modge points at the far section of the infirmary with lots of jars and sacks on shelves and we hurry over.

"There he is!" I call, seeing Shugly's bottom disappearing into a bag of weird orange roots.

Modge reaches in and grabs him and Shugly emerges with his cheeks stuffed full of food like a hamster.

"At least we know what he likes to eat!" Modge says, shoving Shugly back in his pocket and grabbing more roots for later.

While he's stocking up, I hear a noise and discover a gap in the wall behind the shelves. I can't resist having a quick look.

It's like a secret corridor and there are odd noises drifting through. I go a bit further along and find a small room with a glass door. Inside, I can see the vet swearing while he tries to stuff a reluctant creature into a small plastic pod with some force. There are more pods on the shelves, each with a weird creature slumped dejectedly inside. The poor things have all sorts of pipes and tubes

sticking out of them, and are making a variety of sad and miserable noises.

The creatures must be sick, I suppose. Why else would they be keeping them here? But why aren't they in the infirmary with the others?

I want to go in and have a closer look, ask that vet what he's up to, but the glass door is locked when I try it and the electronic keypad is covered in weird symbols that make no sense.

"Danny? Are you coming?" Modge hisses behind me. "The presentation thing's nearly finished!"

I reluctantly turn my back

on the creatures and hurry back down the corridor, trying to convince myself everything is fine. But this place is giving me a very creepy feeling and I'd really like to go home now.

We sit back down in our seats just as the screen goes black and Kaspar and Kaylar come back on the stage, smiling.

"Any questions?" says Kaylar.

"Aye, what's in it for you?" Murgatroyd asks, his moustache bristling.

"Sorry?"

"Well, come on. Surely you're getting something out of it?"

Kaspar's smile slips slightly. "Only the satisfaction of knowing we're making a difference."

"We managed fine before!" grumbles Murgatroyd. "I've been running the IDLPO in Dimension Eflon Icon 78 for fifteen years with no problems. There ain't no need for you to be interfering."

"I can assure you, we wish only to make your lives easier!" Kaspar insists. "Caring for different species for days or weeks and then taking them back to their dimensions in person is inefficient and time-consuming.

"But zooming round a great big rollercoaster and getting licked by thousands of beetles isn't stressful at all, I suppose?" Modge mutters.

"What rollercoaster?" the woman with garden hair asks, turning to look at Modge.

"I can assure you that all the creatures that come through are treated with respect during their short stay with us," Kaspar says quickly, frowning at Modge.

I'm guessing the other caretakers came through the proper way and the creature coaster of doom wasn't part of their tour. Nor was that secret room. Seems to me like half of this whole stupid "tour" is fake.

"Now if that's all —"

"No, it ain't all! I got another question!" Murgatroyd says, ears flapping wildly. I can definitely see why my grandad liked him. "Are you gonna be sticking to creatures?"

"I beg your pardon?"

"Well, if you can sort the creatures out so easy, what's to stop you sorting it all out? All the lost property?" Murgatroyd demands. "Maybe this is just the first step in your grand plan and then we'll all be out of a job!"

A buzz of unhappy voices fills the hall.

Kaylar holds her hands up for quiet, that same annoying, insincere smile still plastered over her face. "We are a Hub for creatures!" she says. "I can assure you we have no grand plan. We want to work together with all of you. We want to help you do your best work and ensure that the system of interdimensional lost property is the very best it can be."

Kaspar continues. "Now if that's all your questions, please head this way and remember to vote in favour for activating a FULL rollout across the multiverse by next Sunday."

"What's happening on Sunday?" Inaaya asks.

"The Delegation from Centralus HQ will be visiting us for a formal tour, before they sign the official contract giving us access to all the IDLPOs in the multiverse," Kaspar replies smoothly. "We look forward to working together with all the caretakers in the future."

Kaspar and Kaylar stand at the door with those weird fixed smiles on their faces and usher the caretakers through.

"Modge, this is it," Inaaya says as the others leave.

"You have to leave Shugly here."

Modge shakes his head. "I don't trust them."

Inaaya frowns. "Danny, tell him."

I pause, catch Modge's eye and see my own worries mirrored there. "He's right. There's something off about this place, Inaaya."

"But we'll get into so much trouble if we're caught!" Inaaya cries, tugging anxiously at her plait.

"We can discuss it later! Let's just go home." I push them both towards the door.

We hurry over to the transport station where the caretakers are using their keys to get zapped back home.

"But Modge," Inaaya whispers in the queue. "How will you look after it? What does it even eat?"

"It's fine, I've got him some food," Modge hisses.

"You found Fligglenog food?" Inaaya says, just a touch too loud.

There's an audible click as two heads suddenly snap in our direction and a second later the Arachnus siblings are crowding around us, way too close, way too desperate.

"Fligglenogs? What do you know about them?" Kaylar demands, her perfect blue eyes searching my face for answers, but there's something . . . something inside them that makes my skin crawl.

"Why are you so interested?" I ask.

"Oh, they're rather rare, that's all. It would be SO wonderful to see one and add it to our records." Kaspar stares at us like a hungry cat about to pounce.

I push my friends closer to the transporter, the need to escape growing stronger with each second. "Well, I'm sure you're in the best place to find one!" I say cheerfully, refusing to crumble.

"Of course," Kaspar says with his shark-like smile in place again. "Please scan your key and you'll be transported back to your IDLPOs at once. Thank you for visiting and we hope you've found it an informative day. Remember, the Hub is here to make your life easier!"

I can feel their creepily perfect eyes on us as I scan Grandad's watch over the pad and step forward. Modge and Inaaya follow me.

Just as the blue light comes to take us, I look back and see 'Centralus Hub Emergency Evacuation System Enterprise' written on the wall in big blue letters. Something about it pings in my head but then we're whooshed back through the transporter and it's gone.

CHAPTER 14

I'd have liked to lie on the floor groaning for A LOT longer, but Modge and Inaaya start arguing about Shugly and I decide to get up so I can kill them both with my bare hands.

"Will you two stop arguing for once! It's driving me mad."

"But Danny," Inaaya says, "you were the one who didn't want your grandad to get in trouble! If they find out Modge has been keeping creatures here, then we'll probably get kicked out and someone else will take over."

"I know what I said, Inaaya, but that was before we went there," I tell her. "Something about that Hub just isn't right."

"Well . . . maybe it's not perfect but it works," Inaaya argues. "You heard how many creatures they've already sent back, clean and healthy."

"But look how horrible the transporter thing was for us," I point out. "Imagine what it feels like for the creatures. And don't you think that rollercoaster thing with the beetle bath must be a bit stressful too?"

"That's it? That's your reason for breaking all the rules? It's a 'bit stressful' for the animals?" Inaaya folds her arms and shakes her head.

"No," I insist. "There was some other weird stuff I saw."

"Weird stuff?" Inaaya scoffs. "Oh, I'm glad to see you've got some solid evidence for your theory."

"I do, actually! There was another room behind the infirmary and they had a few creatures in cages with pipes and tubes sticking out of them and they looked really miserable."

"So? Maybe those animals needed to be quarantined or something," Inaaya says, like I'm an idiot.

I glare at her. "Yeah, well why wasn't that part of the tour then? Or the rollercoaster? Or the beetle thing? They're clearly keeping secrets."

"Oh, you're just being silly now, Danny," she says

with an annoying wave of her hand. "You don't want to upset Modge so you're just making up reasons to let him keep Shugly here."

"I am not!" I insist, ignoring Modge's very obvious and unhelpful wink. "I think there's something funny going on and, until we know for sure, we're keeping Shugly here where it's safe."

"And how are you going to know 'for sure'?" Inaaya's hands are on her hips now.

"We're going to . . . ummm . . ." My mind has gone blank under my cousin's laser-like stare.

"Investigate!" Modge shouts.

"Yes!" I agree, loudly. "Exactly. Investigate. We're going to look into the whole Hub thing. And if we find anything, we'll report it to Mrs A and she can deal with it."

"And I can look after Shugly while we investigate. I've already found the food he likes." Modge says, emptying his pockets on to the table.

"And what are you doing to do when that runs out?" Inaaya asks. "It needs to go back to its own dimension. That's what's best for it, Modge."

Modge points his finger at Inaaya. "Don't pretend

you care about Shugly! You just don't want to get into trouble!"

"I don't want ANY of us to get in trouble, what's wrong with that? I thought your grandad asked you to look after things, Danny," Inaaya says to me. "Surely he meant keep things running like they're supposed to?"

I bite my lip. I really, really don't want to let my grandad down, but I won't force Modge to send Shugly to that horrible place and Miss Bossy Face can't make me.

"Oh, keep your pants on, Inaaya!" I flop down in the big dragon-skin chair. "I'm sure we can keep Shugly secret till my grandad comes back and then he can decide. It's not like anyone else comes here except us."

At that EXACT moment the outside door beeps and a deep sense of panic swamps me. Mrs Arburknuckle! Aargh! Why hadn't I remembered her love of surprise visits? If she finds Shugly here, we're all for the chop – and worst of all, Inaaya will hold this over me forever.

"Quick! There's someone here. Hide!" I hiss at Modge while desperately ignoring Inaaya's patented and hugely annoying smug face.

"Where?" Modge asks, clutching Shugly to his chest.

"I don't know!"

Inaaya sighs at our ineptitude, tugs the cleaning cupboard open and shoves Modge and Shugly inside.

"Just try and act normal," she says to me as we go through to the office to meet Mrs Arburknuckle.

But instead of a squid on a Segway, it's a short hairy man wearing combat trousers and boots, with weird telescope glasses covering his eyes. He's got wiry orange hair covering his chest like a shirt and a leather shoulder holster strapped around his shoulders.

"I'm IDLPO Inspector Echelon Xanadu of the Dimension Xargle Blarg 12," he says in a flat, raspy voice.

"Who?"

"I SAID, I'M THE IDLPO INSPECTOR, ECHELON XANADU," he shouts.

Echelon Xanadu? I try not to laugh at the name.

"I'm here to inspect this office and make sure you're not infringing any of the rules."

He thrusts a piece of paper into my hands. It's covered in official writing with a big seal on the bottom. My belly rolls over. A Lost Property Inspection? NOW? How's that for bad timing?

"What sort of infringements are you looking for?" I ask, trying not to sound guilty in any way.

Echelon sniffs and whips a thick notebook from his holster. "Improper record keeping, untidy work spaces, souvenir keeping, breaking hygiene regulations . . ."

He starts strolling around the office, his telescope glasses zooming in and out. I wonder exactly how many rules we're already breaking, apart from hiding an alien creature.

"Your job must be well boring," I say, trying to sound super casual.

Echelon glares at me. "Actually, we uncover

some VERY serious crimes in our work. We're a very FASTIDIOUS department. Nothing gets past us, you know. Black market profiteering for example, or failing to comply with the new regulations regarding the proper procedures for live creatures."

I hold his gaze, trying not to let my panic show. Is he psychic or something?

He moves closer, his weird telescope lenses zooming in on my face. "Keeping live creatures in a lost property office within the trial area, for example, could lead to VERY SERIOUS PUNISHMENTS. Instant dismissal would be the least you could expect."

"And how often do you do these inspections?" Inaaya asks, taking the official paper from my hand and scanning it with her eyes.

"As often as we need to, missy!" Echelon snaps, glaring at Inaaya instead. "Now if you'd just move out of my way and let me get to work . . ."

Fudgety fudge bombs! He's going to find Modge and then he'll find Shugly and then we'll all be arrested and sent to some grotty space jail forever and worst of all, I'll have to live with Inaaya saying she told me so every day for the next ninety-seven years!

"I'm afraid we can't do that," Inaaya says with all the calmness of a yoga teacher.

"Interfering with an official inspection is a crime!" Echelon claims.

"But this isn't an official inspection, is it?"

He falters. "What?"

Inaaya holds up the paper he gave us. "According to this document, standard inspections require forty-eight hours' written notice, which we have not received. Therefore I believe you are contravening your powers."

"What?" Echelon Xanadu says again.

"You heard me!" Inaaya folds her arms and lifts her chin. "If you continue this unofficial inspection I will report you, as is my right according to this document you provided."

Echelon looks like he's about to explode. "You realise this behaviour makes you look MORE suspicious?" he snarls. "What are you hiding? Hand it over now or they'll be terrible consequences. You can't hide anything from us. Our fastidiousness knows no bounds. We won't be stopped!"

Inaaya doesn't let his tantrum phase her. "IF you

had ANY actual evidence you'd have a warrant to search the place immediately, but you don't have one of those, do you? You're attempting to do an unlicensed inspection for some reason, but it's not legal. So I suggest you leave now before I report you."

Echelon grits his teeth. "Fine then, missy. I'll leave. But I'll be back in EXACTLY forty-eight hours, and believe me – I will search this entire IDLPO from top to bottom and ANY infraction will be reported. Do you understand?"

Inaaya smiles. "It seems like you're the one who doesn't understand the rules of his own office, Mr Xanadu."

Practically growling, Echelon slams out of the office and disappears in a flash of blue light.

Inaaya lets out a shuddering breath.

I stare at my cousin with new-found respect. "THAT was the coolest thing I've ever seen."

"And that might be the first nice thing you've ever said to me," she says, looking surprised.

"Seriously though," I say. "Are you sure you want to be a space scientist thingy? I think you should consider a career as a lawyer because you totally smoked his butt."

Inaaya shrugs. "Maybe I'll do both."

"It's a bit weird, isn't it?" I ask. "Him turning up like that?"

She shrugs. "If you give some people a little bit of power, they always try and abuse it. Anyway, we're going to have to get Shugly out of here before that colossal wombat comes back AND we have to make sure there's nothing else we can get into trouble for. I don't fancy being stuck in a jail cell with you two idiots."

"Yeah, well we wouldn't want to be stuck with a bossy pants like you either!" Suddenly I remember we've left Modge stuck in the cupboard for ages. "Let's get Modge out and make a plan."

I yank open the door but there's no sign of Modge. He's vanished and taken Shugly with him. Which means that I've somehow managed to LOSE my best friend in an actual LOST property office.

You have to admit that takes talent.

CHAPTER 15

"Modge? MODGE!" I shove buckets and mops aside but he's not hiding. "He's definitely not in here."

"What?" says Inaaya. "Where did he go?"

"How should I know? I was with you the whole time!"

Inaaya pushes me aside and moves the exact same mops and buckets. "He's not here."

"I just told you that!"

"But where could he be?"

"Maybe Shugly kidnapped him?" I suggest.

"Don't be ridiculous!" Inaaya snaps.

"Why is that more ridiculous than an interdimensional lost property office, a squid on a Segway or any of the billion other mad things that have happened?"

"Because why would ANYONE kidnap

Modge?" Inaaya says. "He's practically useless."

"Oi! Modge is my best friend, you know. And he might not be perfect but I think he's pretty cool actually."

"Of course you do," Inaaya says. "He thinks you're the best thing since sliced bread so you're bound to like him."

"Maybe I AM the best thing since sliced bread! Maybe you just don't appreciate me!"

"I'd appreciate it if you'd just shut up and find your stupid friend!"

We're so busy glaring at each other we don't notice the back of the cupboard move, until Modge pops out and makes us both jump.

"Danny, you're not going to believe this!" He's practically buzzing.

"Where have you been?" I demand.

"Oh, I found this door in the back of the cupboard and look it leads down to –"

"You shouldn't just disappear, Modge!" Inaaya says.

"Yes, but you need to come and see –"

Inaaya carries on telling him off. "We had a visit

from a very disagreeable lost property office inspector and he's going to come back soon, so we need to send Shugly to the hub quickly before we all get arrested!"

"It's not just Shugly we need to worry about anymore!" Modge shouts, which finally shuts her up.

"What?"

"Come on!" Modge disappears again, and this time Inaaya and I follow him through the door in the back of the cupboard and down a set of stairs into a large white room.

It takes me a minute or two to make sense of what I can see.

Around twenty large glass pods line the room and about six of them are filled with creatures . . .

"See?" says Modge. "Your grandad hasn't been sending them to the Hub either, Danny! He's been carrying on like before and keeping them down here in the creature bay."

Like a heavy thud in my brain, the promise I made to 'look after them' suddenly makes sense. Except I hadn't looked after them. I didn't even know they were here! How could I have known? My grandad never said they were hidden in the back of a poxy

cupboard. I mean, I know he was having a heart attack at the time, but it might have been useful.

"Are they all okay?" I ask Modge.

"Yeah, it's a pretty clever system really," he says. "They get food and water through a little door up there, see?" He points to a feeder system above each pod that seems to be adjusted for each creature. "I've topped the stores up now so they'll be fine for a few days. I think they were a bit lonely but they perked up when I came down."

"Your grandad broke the rules?" Inaaya asks me, her eyes round with shock. "He kept all these creatures down here instead of sending them to the Hub? What was he thinking?"

"The same as me and Danny probably," Modge says. "That the Hub can't be trusted."

"But . . . he can't just keep them here!"

"I don't think he was keeping them in here permanently," Modge says. "Look, this is a CAT." He points to a small yellow rocket-shaped machine stationed in an alcove in the wall.

"No, it's not!" I tell him, still feeling a bit dazed. "Cats have more fur and more claws."

Modge laughs. "No, you muppet. A C.A.T.! A Creature Astrovial Transporter. This is what the caretakers used to take the creatures back to their dimensions before the Hub existed. I think your grandad just kept using it."

I swallow. I can't believe there's even MORE stuff Grandad never told me. "How do you know all this, Modge?"

"It's all up here, on this board." He points at a large pin board on the wall, full of bits of paper and lists. "He wrote down all the creatures, when they arrived, when he took them back, where he took them. Everything."

I peer closer, reading my grandad's writing.

"I think he must have got behind with taking them back because there's a big gap at the end," Modge says. "So they all built up down here and then he had a heart attack, so . . ."

I shake my head. This was all my fault. I should have been here more. I should have been more reliable. Then maybe Grandad would have told me about his other job instead of trying to do everything himself.

"What are we going to do?" Even I can hear the panic in my voice. "We might have been able to hide

Shugly but we can't hide all this!" I fling my arms around to encompass the whole room. "Echelon will find them, my grandad will get the sack, we'll get into loads of trouble and they'll send all the creatures to the stupid, evil Hub!"

"Well . . . we'll just have to take them all back for him," Modge says.

"Wait. You think WE should use that rocket thing to travel to different dimensions?" I ask, staring at Modge in shock.

Modge shrugs. "I reckon we could have a go. It can't be that hard."

Inaaya stops her frantic pacing. "Of course it can! It's interdimensional space travel!" She bellows. "It's not something you can just 'have a go' at. We could get lost, we could get the coordinates wrong and end up stuck between two dimensions, we could blow up on take-off or land in the middle of a giant acid monster lake, or something!"

Modge sniffs. "Danny's grandad did it all the time."

"Well, he probably had some training first!"

"There's an instruction book in the cockpit," Modge says.

Inaaya throws her hands in the air. "Oh, well, that's all right then. I suppose you think astronauts just read a few books and then boom, flew right to the moon!"

Modge rolls his eyes, which sets Inaaya off on another rant.

"But even if we could fly that weird, rickety rocket to different dimensions, we could never do it in time. That ridiculous inspector Echelon is coming back in two days! It would be impossible to take all these creatures back in time. We only get a few hours here every day!"

"What other choice is there?" I ask, slowly realising this is our only option, however mad it sounds. "Go to space prison? Get my grandad in trouble too? And risk the creatures falling into the wrong hands?"

"We've got no proof the Hub is up to anything," Inaaya says through tightly gritted teeth. "I admit some of their methods aren't great, but you saw their success rate!"

"But how do we even know it's true? They could be lying," Modge says.

"Why would they lie?"

"My grandad wouldn't do all this for nothing," I insist. "He must have had a good reason."

"But what, Danny?" Inaaya asks. Her voice is getting louder. "What terrible things do you think the people who donated an entire creature welfare Hub to the multiverse are doing?"

"I don't know! Maybe they're selling creatures to the black market? That inspector said that was a thing!"

Inaaya frowns. "But what for? They're already billionaires, they don't need more money."

Why does Inaaya have to be right all the time? It's so annoying.

"Well . . ." I flounder on. "There's SOMETHING fishy going on. I know there is."

"Danny, this is madness," Inaaya says slowly, like she's talking to a five year old. "Let's just send all the creatures to the Hub. That's the sensible thing to do. The responsible thing."

"Danny, no, you can't trust them!" Modge insists, clutching Shugly to his chest. "I don't mind if Shugly goes home, to his real home where he'll be safe, but I'm not giving him to the Hub! You saw how weird they were about Fligglenogs."

This is ridiculous. We're just going round in circles. If only my grandad had told me something useful instead of whiffling on about cheese! He doesn't even like cheese!

A spark of a memory jabs at me.

"Wait," I tell Modge and Inaaya. It all suddenly connects in my brain. "CHEESE!" I shout. "Beware the Cheese!"

Modge and Inaaya gape at me with wide open mouths, like two fat trouts hanging on a hook while I do my epic victory dance.

"Are you feeling okay, Danny?" Modge asks. "Maybe you should lie down."

"I'm not going mad!" I stop dancing so I can share my brilliant realisation. "When my grandad had his heart attack, one of the things he said to me was 'beware the cheese'. I thought it was nonsense but it's not."

"Isn't it?"

"No!" I yell. "I just realised CHEESE are the initials for Centralus Hub Emergency Evacuation System Enterprise! I saw it written on the wall of the Hub when we left but I didn't put it together till just now."

"He's right," Inaaya says slowly.

"I know I am! My grandad was warning me about the Hub! Beware the Cheese means beware the

- *152* -

Hub! He wanted me to look after the creatures AND keep them away from the Hub!" I feel lighter all of a sudden. Now I know what my grandad actually wanted, I can make the right decisions.

"But you can't keep them here, Danny," Inaaya reminds me. "Not with Echelon coming in two days."

I nod. "You're right. We can't. We'll have to take them all back. That's what my grandad was going to do. We can do this, Inaaya. I know we can."

Inaaya starts shaking her head. "Don't say we. I won't be a part of it. It's madness. Zipping around the multiverse in a rusty old rocket dropping off creatures is bad enough, but trying to do it all in just two days is ridiculous!"

"Not if we tell our parents we're having a sleepover this weekend," I say, warming to the idea. "There's only five or six creatures. We'll have loads of time if we don't have to go home in between."

"It'll be well fun!" Modge says, totally over excited by the idea already. "We can bring sleeping bags and get loads of snacks from the shop and I can keep Shugly company. He'll like that." He squeezes Shugly, who squirms happily in his hands and lets out a small cheep.

"Yeah, we haven't had a sleepover for ages," I agree. It would be good to get away for a few days, actually. Being at home without Mum there nagging and moaning just makes me miss her even more, and Aunt Rekha's endless frantic cooking and cleaning is doing my head in.

"Well, I suppose I'll be able to get all my homework done without you two there to annoy me. My astrology report is well overdue," Inaaya says but her eyes keep darting over to the rocket.

"Yeah, I'm sure homework will be loads of fun," I say. "Not quite as exciting as becoming interdimensional explorers like me and Modge, and seeing remarkable things that no one else in the world will ever see . . ."

Inaaya's fidgeting and chewing at the end of her plait now, so I keep talking because we need her. If that rocket manual is anything like the other one, I won't have a chance of understanding it.

"I mean, this is probably a once in a lifetime opportunity," I ramble on, "especially for someone who wants to be an astrophysicist but you have to do what you think best. Modge, you tell your dad you're staying at mine, I'll tell my dad I'm staying at yours –"

"And I'll tell my mum I have a residential study club at school," Inaaya says quickly.

"What?"

"I can't possibly let you two go off on your own," Inaaya points out. "Who knows how much trouble you'd cause? If you insist on going, then the responsible thing for me to do is come with you and make sure it all goes smoothly."

"Oh, well, that's very kind of you, Inaaya," I say, filled with giddy relief which I'm obviously not going to show Inaaya. "Isn't that kind, Modge?"

"I suppose so," Modge says reluctantly.

I can see he'd rather go without Inaaya but that's because he probably thinks being trapped forever in a crazy doom dimension with his weird new pet would be fun. I, on the other hand, would quite like to come home again and Inaaya's our best chance of that happening.

Inaaya shrugs. "We all have to do our duty."

"Yeah, yeah. Calm down, Mother Theresa," Modge says under his breath, and I pretend my laugh is a cough.

CHAPTER 16

"It's VERY important!" Inaaya tells me, staring deep into my eyes as she hands over the notebook and pen like it's holy treasure. "You have to document EVERYTHING. This is how research is done, Danny, with attention to detail. I need this for my future work but I'll be too busy making sure we don't get lost in another dimension FOREVER to fill it in properly, so I'm trusting you to do a good job."

I frown. "Are you sure you should be keeping notes?"

"It's fine," Inaaya soothes. "I keep the book here all the time so no one else will find it. I need to keep meticulous notes so I can use what I learn to discover everything I can about the dimensional realities and how they relate to each other."

"All right, chillax, Inaaya. We're not at school now."

"Do NOT let me down," she practically hisses.

I shake my head as she stalks off. Fine, if she wants detail, I'll give her poxy detail.

INAAYA's ASTROPHYSICIST NOTEBOOK
VERY PRIVATE. DO NOT READ! NOT EVER!!!

Friday 6.30 p.m.
Modge, Inaaya and me enter the IDLPO and get ready for our grand adventures.

Friday 6.45 p.m.
Inaaya starts reading the entire manual for the CAT. Me and Modge sit behind the controls and pretend to drive it with added sound effects and crashes.

Friday 7.30 p.m.
Inaaya reads the info cards on all the creature pods and notes down the relevant dimensional coordinates to input into the CAT as needed, while me and Modge make a special nest for Shugly to fit in the CAT.

Friday 8 p.m.
Inaaya writes long boring lists and whiffles on about rules and being careful, while me and Modge eat most of the food supplies that are supposed to last us all weekend.

Friday 9 p.m.
Inaaya insists we all go to bed so we are ready nice and early tomorrow.

Friday 10 p.m.
"SHUT UP!" Inaaya shouts at me and Modge because we're reading comics with torches under our sleeping bags and giggling.

Friday 10.04 p.m.
"GO TO SLEEP!" Inaaya shouts.

Friday 10.07 p.m.
"I'm warning you!" Inaaya yells but this only makes me and Modge giggle more.

Friday 10.38 p.m.

Modge and me fall asleep. Inaaya stays up worrying. (PROBABLY.)

Saturday 7.30 A.M!

"Time to get up!" Inaaya shouts WAY TOO EARLY, kicking our sleeping bags until we open our eyes and then kicking them again by 'accident'. "Get up now or I'm going to start singing!"

I cover my head with my pillow but she starts singing the soundtrack to *Frozen* at the top of her lungs and the horrific noise penetrates everything and drills into my brain. Me and Modge get up, which is annoying but at least Inaaya stops singing. While she checks her lists AGAIN, Modge and me eat a healthy breakfast (doughnuts followed by Haribo).

Inaaya triple-checks her lists and packs the CAT with a medical kit and survival supplies in case of emergency.

Modge adds three jumbo packs of Monster Munch and four family packs of biscuits in case of a REAL emergency and then finally, we're ready to go!

Saturday 9.30 a.m.

**** DRUM ROLL ****

COMMENCE THE GREAT CREATURE RETURN PLAN!!

I fit pod number 1 - containing a green star-shaped creature called a Schnurder - into the back of the CAT with Modge and Shugly.

Inaaya types the origin wyrm hole coordinates into the CAT.

Inaaya and me argue over who sits in the pilot chair but I win easily by sitting in the pilot chair first and refusing to move.

Saturday 9.45 a.m.

LAUNCH to Dimension!

Saturday 9.46 a.m.

Launch cancelled due to Modge needing the toilet. Inaaya swears quite impressively. I'm glad they learn something useful at that private school of hers.

(This is **NOT** the detail I was talking about and you know it Danny Dourado! My astrophysicist notebook is a place for **SCIENCE** not **NONSENSE**. Please desist from such silliness in future entries. I.M.)

(IF YOU SAY SO! D.D.)

Saturday 10.05 a.m.

LAUNCH to Dimension SKZV! Take two!

observations by Danny Dourado

ENVIRONMENT – thick jungle, massive trees, vines, flowers and the sound of birds and insects EVERYWHERE.

SMELL – like the locker room at the swimming pool – damp and hot with the pungent whiff of a hundred different deodorants fighting for attention.

MISSION – successful.

(Danny! We need much more detail than this! I.M.)

(Oh, make your flipping mind up! D.D.)

Okay so THIS is what ACTUALLY HAPPENS.

The rocket shudders for a minute, then zooms like a Ferrari towards the office wall. Just before impact, and before I can finish screaming, the wall disappears and so does everything else. Beyond the windscreen there's only a speckled black that goes on and on and on until we burst through some sort of glowing window and landed rather bumpily in a forest.

A calm voice from the rocket computer says, "Dimension SZX. Beware flying Zurgon berries which explode on impact."

"Hurry up Modge," Inaaya instructs.

"All right, calm down," Modge grumps, pushing the button to open the CAT's sliding doors. Only they don't open. Instead a light starts flashing on the wall and a small compartment opens up to reveal three glass tubes full of some sort of brown ooze with green flecks floating in it.

The rocket voice says, "Please take your monthly atmospheric adjustment juice before opening the door to avoid instant death."

"What the flip is atmospheric adjustment juice and why does it look like that?" I demand.

"I suppose other dimensions may have different atmospheres and drinking this . . . juice . . . must adjust our bodies somehow so we can breathe," Inaaya says.

"We're supposed to drink it?" I ask, feeling a bit sick already.

"Unless you'd prefer instant death?" she says, picking up her tube.

"Maybe I would," I say, staring at the noxious juice.

"How bad can it be?" Modge asks, passing me a tube and grabbing his own. "All together now."

I tip my head back and try not to think about what I'm pouring in. The goo hits my tongue and covers it with a rancid bitter slime that slides down my throat, burning and fizzing as it goes. I can feel my lungs spasm, making me cough and cough till my chest aches.

"Urgh. I think instant death might have been better," I gasp.

Modge grins at me. "Not as bad as school custard though."

Inaaya wipes her mouth with the back of her hand and swallows hard, keeping the rancid contents down through sheer stubbornness.

"Try the doors again, Modge!" she commands.

This time they slide open straight away.

Modge climbs out and I help him heave the Schnurder out of the cage. Modge has only gone two steps when a rampant yellow vine starts winding round his leg.

"Modge, put that creature down and get back here now," I tell him.

"All right, give us a chance."

Modge bends down to release the Schnurder gently into the grass and it digs itself into the soft ground

within seconds. But when Modge tries to make his way back to us, the vine tightens on his leg and small fanged flowers emerge and start chomping at his ankle.

Modge lets out a scream, so I jump out of the rocket and go pelting towards him on a rescue mission. I stamp on the vines, grab my mate and drag him back to the rocket while Zurgon berries fall from the trees around us, exploding like fruity grenades, making it feel like we're in a real-life battlefield.

We dive back into the rocket. Inaaya shuts the door, presses the home button on the control panel and whooshes us back to the IDLPO.

"Are you okay?" I demand of Modge once we're back.

"I think so." He looks down at his trouser leg where the material has been frayed to holes by the flowers' gnashing teeth. Another minute and they'd have been at his flesh.

"I think leaving the rocket might be a bad idea," Inaaya says.

"So we just chuck the creatures out the door?" Modge asks, soothing Shugly who's nestled into his neck, trembling slightly.

"It'll save time," I tell him.

"That's a good thing," Inaaya says. "That trip took us ages."

It only felt like ten minutes. According to the clock though, it's somehow been over two hours since we left.

Inaaya fiddles with the CAT's control panel. "There must be a time lag when we travel this way. I think the technology is quite dated compared to the transporter beam they use at the Hub."

"At least it doesn't make you feel like you've been trapped in a tumble drier for three days," Modge says, which is true enough. The effects of travelling by CAT are much gentler.

"Hopefully we'll still have enough time to get them all home," says Inaaya.

I cross my fingers. Nothing else we can do now but try.

Saturday 1 p.m.
Dimension ZUFF95x
Creature – Apeynor Meng X

Touchdown is a bit smoother this time but there's nothing but black beyond the windscreen. Modge wants to know if it's night-time but maybe it's like this ALL the time? I tell him to just be careful and open the door.

ENVIRONMENT – no idea. can't see anything.
   SMELLS – like sulphur. Cold, wet breeze. The sound of flapping wings and shrieking fills the air.

The small black and silver creature in the pod unfurls itself from a tight ball and shrieks so loud I think my ears might pop.

"Quick!" Inaaya shouts.

The shrieking from outside gets louder and louder as if responding to the creature's cries. Modge fumbles with the lid but finally snaps it open and the Apeynor Meng X is gone, flown away on gossamer wings to join its family.

I shut the doors and we travel back to the IDLPO.

Saturday 4.50 p.m.
Dimension WWWWW8
Creature – Zxdericous Parp

ENVIRONMENT - for the first time we land near a city, though the buildings in the distance look like they're made from rainbow-coloured sand that sparkles in the pink light coming from their sun. Instead of roads, there are rivers running through everything that flow like thick orange chocolate, with small boats shaped like the shells of coconuts bobbing about.

WEATHER - warm, gentle breeze.

SMELLS - like cinnamon and oranges and pine needles.

CHAPTER 17

Inaaya ripped this next page out but I think it's important to include ALL the facts for . . . umm . . . scientific reasons.

"WOW!" Inaaya stares out the windscreen with a hungry expression. "Look at this place!"

"It is amazing," I agree.

"We could get out here, I think," she says. "It looks perfectly safe."

"We don't have time, Inaaya."

"Just for a minute," she begs.

"No. Just let the creature out and let's go."

Modge grabs the pod and the one-eyed blob inside quivers with excitement. I open the door, Modge opens the pod – but the creature inside doesn't even move. Modge gives the pod a shake but the Zxdericous

Parp doesn't take the hint.

"I'll have to get out to tip him out," Modge says reluctantly.

"I'll do it!" Inaaya says.

Before I can stop her she grabs the pod and leaps outside. She takes a few steps on to the glowing blue grass, staring around her as she goes, trying to absorb everything she can.

"Inaaya!" I hiss after a minute.

"All right," she snaps, bending down with the pod and tipping the creature on to the grass.

The Zxdericous Parp suddenly swells up like a balloon and then releases a huge cloud of gas that sends it shooting fifty foot forward, engulfing Inaaya in a mustard yellow fog that makes her cough.

Modge and me are laughing too much to help her as she stumbles back towards us, still coughing, her clothes and hair stained yellow.

"I guess we know where its name came from," Modge splutters as Inaaya climbs in, and I think she's going to hit him so I shut the door and zap us away, still snorting.

I go to the chip shop for dinner and Inaaya's still in the toilet when I get back.

Modge pounces on the food and we divvy it up on to paper plates. It's possible Inaaya's portion is a smidge smaller than ours but it's her own fault for not coming out even after I yelled for her three times.

Finally, when Modge and me are snaffling up the crispy bits of chips from the paper, Inaaya comes out. She's less yellow than before but a faint farty smell still surrounds her. Judging by her face though I don't think it's safe to mention it.

"I'm going to have to go home for a bath," she says.

"You can't. You told your mum you were staying at school."

"I know but I can't bear it! The soap in the bathroom is rubbish. I need better stuff to get rid of the smell."

"You'll get used to it," Modge says, rubbing Shugly's tummy while he purrs. "Remember that time I rolled in fox poo in the park when we went camping, Danny? After a couple of days I couldn't even smell it any more."

Inaaya makes a face and sits down with her slightly depleted dinner. "Well, I think the Hub is a great idea if it avoids all this horribleness."

I gape at her. "But you loved seeing that last place! You'd have missed all of that."

"I'm not sure it's worth stinking like a cesspit for days," Inaaya grumbles. "What sort of dimension has creatures that travel by fart power?"

"Maybe that's the future, Inaaya," I say. "Maybe the whole multiverse will be powered by farts one day."

Modge laughs. "That would be cool."

"Ugh, no, it wouldn't!"

I grin. "Well, I think this is a much better system than the Hub. Better for the creatures and way more interesting for the Caretakers. I can see why my grandad does it now."

"Yeah, it's really nice to see the creatures go back to their own homes." Modge says cheerfully.

"Yeah, you can see how happy they are."

"It's always nice to go home though." I say. "I miss my bed and my room and all my stuff, and I've only been gone a day."

"Me too," Modge says. "The best thing about going

away is when you go back home at the end of it."

Inaaya stabs viciously at her chips with her wooden fork, her face like a thundercloud.

"Cheer up, Inaaya. We've only got three more trips to do," I tell her.

"I don't want to cheer up! I'm behind with all my homework and my astronomy project, I lied to my mum, I'm stuck in here with you two and I smell disgusting!"

"Yeah, but you always smell disgusting," Modge jokes.

Inaaya throws a chip at him which hits him smack on the forehead before he picks it up, dunks it in ketchup and eats it. I'm pretty sure I hear Inaaya mumble something about "Neanderthals" under her breath but I can't be sure.

We all fall asleep really quickly but I'm still exhausted in the morning, as if bouncing around the multiverse all day has taken a toll. I'm not looking forward to doing it all again today, but I can't moan, seeing as we're doing all this to save my grandad's job.

Inaaya nibbles at a nut bar while me and Modge inhale a pack of doughnuts to try and get enough energy to get out of our sleeping bags.

"Come on then!" Inaaya says, clapping her hands together like an over-enthusiastic nursery teacher. "We've got a really busy day."

I yawn and force myself to get up and dressed. Then I stagger into the rocket, still yawning and half awake. It's possible I've forgotten something important but it's too late now.

Dear Ian,

My mate Danny forgot to bring you on our last trip, so I said I'd write up what happened cos I've got a really good memory and also I don't think it's fair if only Inaaya and Danny get to write in you. There are THREE of us so we should all get a turn.

So Ian, what happened was we took off in the CAT and a second later arrived in this other dimension! Just like that! AMAZING or what? It's all pretty cool really, travelling around the multiverse, and doesn't actually seem that tricky despite Inaaya making a MASSIVE fuss about it.

We landed in a big gloopy swamp and it took a while for the transporter legs to stabilise. Outside it was raining these big fat gobbets of yellow mud that ran slowly down the windows.

When we opened the door it smelled a bit like someone had mixed mouldy bananas and rotten fish together, and then boiled it for a month so the steaming wet stink of it was everywhere.

Honestly, it was proper YUCKY, Ian. It was even worse than the smell from the bin sheds on our estate last summer when there was a heat wave.

Anyway, I grabbed the pod with the Gurble in it while Inaaya turned slowly green, Danny coughed and choked and Shugly stuck his head in my armpit to avoid it.

I guess the smell must have woken the Gurble up because it went from being flat and still to puffing up like a puffer fish and boinging around the pod like a mad thing. It was quite cute really. I liked the way its little flipper feet wiggled when it bounced.

"Hurry up, Modge!" Inaaya said, being a massive bossy pants as usual.

I ignored her as usual.

Danny helped me move the pod to the edge of the door and when I opened the door the Gurble boinged outside and landed in the mud with a big fat splat.

As the door closed I spotted a GIANT Gurble emerge from the sludgy mud and open its mouth really wide like a snake when it swallows an egg.

"AW, look! That must be his mum!" I said, pointing it out to Danny.

"I hope so," Danny said under his breath as our little Gurble boinged straight inside the big Gurble's mouth.

I'm pretty sure it was though. Probably all his brothers and sisters were inside too and their mum was keeping them all safe inside her mouth.

Danny shut the door and Inaaya launched the CAT to take us back to the IDLPO, and I felt a bit sad that I'd never see that little gurble again. I was glad he was with his mum though.

That's all for now Ian!

See you later,

Modge

(DANNY I DID NOT GIVE YOU PERMISSION TO LET MODGE WRITE IN MY NOTEBOOK! And WHY is he writing to IAN? WHO IS IAN? This is supposed to be a scientific journal, please STOP filling it with your ridiculous nonsense!! I.M.)

(Oh, calm down! You're the one who called your notebook IAN! Just look at the INITIALS on the front! And I think Modge did a good job, actually, it's way more interesting than all your boring science stuff, so there! D.D.)

(I shall be writing the entries from NOW ON! You two clearly can't be trusted! I.M.)

(Fine. I hope you and Ian are very happy together! D.D.)

(Oh shut up! I.M.)

When we get back to the IDLPO Inaaya goes upstairs to the loo and comes back looking even more stressed than usual.

"The net's nearly full!" she says. "We'll have to clear it before we can do any more trips."

"Have we got time?" I ask.

"If Modge and I clear the net and you get everything ready for our trip, we might manage it."

Modge rolls his eyes at me but stomps up the stairs behind Inaaya. I get on with clearing out the rocket and preparing the pod for the next creature and imagine my grandad having to do the same thing every day all by himself.

I stare over at the big board on the wall that charts all of his illegal trips across the multiverse. What made him break the rules? What made him NOT trust the Hub enough to risk his job?

I wonder if he's got some evidence somewhere of what they're really up to? Maybe we can use that to stop Centralus expanding the trial across the multiverse!

I paw through the pinned papers a bit too enthusiastically and half of them fall on the floor, but that just reveals a whole layer of other papers. My eye is drawn to an official looking letter from Centralus and pretty soon I'm lost.

"Danny? What have you been doing?" Inaaya demands when they return and find me sitting in a pile of paper.

"Investigating."

Inaaya frowns. "You were supposed to be preparing!"

"What did you find out?" Modge asks, grabbing a handful of those weird orange roots from the stores and feeding them to Shugly.

"Well, Grandad's been suspicious since it all began. Look, he's cut out all these clippings about the Hub." I hold them up so they can see. "He sent letters to Centralus asking for more information about the Hub, about what would happen to the creatures, about Kaspar and Kaylar's background."

"And?"

"And nothing! They said there was nothing suspicious to find. But they're wrong!"

"Danny —" Inaaya says with a long-suffering sigh.

"Why did Kaspar and Kaylar Arachnus make a Hub for the IDLPO?" I demand. "If they wanted to be generous, why not donate loads of money to the hungry or the homeless or saving the elephants or something? Don't you think it's weird, wanting to spend millions on something that was already working fine?"

Inaaya shrugs. "But none of this is evidence. So far your 'investigation' hasn't proved anything."

She marches off to the bathroom, leaving me fuming. Mainly because she's right. Again. There's no EVIDENCE. I've no idea why my grandad had broken the rules, and I have nothing to convince the Centralus delegation not to expand the trial.

Modge slaps me on the shoulder. "Don't worry, mate. We'll uncover the truth about them and then Anooya will have to admit she's wrong."

"Or maybe we're the ones who're wrong?" I suggest, flopping down on a chair, my certainty draining away.

"No way. Your grandad didn't trust them and neither should we!"

Modge passes me a pack of doughnuts and I stuff one in my mouth.

"You know, I don't think doing so many trips at once was a good idea," Modge says, through a mouthful of doughnut. "I feel like I've done ten laps of the school field in the rain."

"We don't have any choice. That stupid Echelon Xanadu is coming back this evening and we have to get rid of all the creatures," Inaaya grumbles, coming back from the bathroom.

"There's only one trip left," I point out.

"Two trips!" Inaaya says. "Don't forget Shugly needs to go back."

"I know," Modge says, letting the fluffy ball lick at his sugary finger with a delicate purple tongue. "But we can do him last, can't we?"

Inaaya sighs. "I suppose so. But it has to be done. He doesn't belong here with us."

Shugly purrs and nuzzles Modge's hand which makes me wonder if somehow they were meant to find each other.

Despite feeling overtired and stressed about the imminent return of the IDPLO inspector, I can't deny a bit of excitement at what dimensions we might see today. The small glimpses are so tantalising, you can't help imagining what those worlds are like.

CHAPTER 18

Inaaya

Sunday 11.30 a.m.

Takeoff

Dimension - Squefflezz Qnimitz [2 digits]

Creature - Weg

The rocket lands in an ocean of endless yellow water but due to its buoyancy the rocket floats well.

Outside the sky is purple with black thunder clouds sparking above us, which leads me to wonder about how much the weather systems differ between dimensions.

(NOTE - Keep accurate records of weather in each dimension so they can be compared.)

Modge slides open the flap in the rocket roof and shoves the open pod through just as the water around us starts churning and something large and quite likely hungry begins to circle us.

(**NOTE** – Wonder how dangerous the creatures in other dimensions are compared to ours?)

The disc-shaped Weg wriggles out of the pod and slides into the water.

"He's gone! Let's get out of here," Danny says as if I am somehow incapable of realising such a thing myself. I hold in a sigh and hit the button but nothing happens.

"Inaaya!" Danny yells with his usual lack of control.

"It's not working." I inform him calmly, keeping one eye on the creature circling us, while I try the button again. Nothing happens. I check all of the instruments but can't see a problem.

Modge shuts the roof flap and sits down. "What's up?" he asks.

"The stupid rocket's not working!" Danny says, banging his fist down on the control panel like a barbarian.

"Stop that!" I shout, concerned he might break something.

"That's what my dad always does when

something's broken!"

"Well, it hasn't worked, has it?"

Danny shrugs. "Maybe it's a special thing only dads can do?" he says, which is a ridiculous notion but I don't have the time to tell him so.

"It's getting closer!" Modge says, his nose pressed against the window.

"What is?"

"Whatever that thing is in the water!"

I peer out of the windscreen to confirm this information.

"This is NOT good," I officially inform the crew while trying to stave off the adrenalin rushing through my system.

"Try turning it off and on again?" Modge suggests and even though I know this is most likely pointless I do it anyway.

As I predicted nothing happens. One glance through the window reveals the circling creature rising up from the sea, displaying sharp golden spike fins and a huge segmented tail.

(NOTE - Look up aquatic dinosaurs and see if a similar species can be found.)

I grab the instruction book and begin turning pages as fast as possible in an attempt to find the answer to our current predicament.

Danny slams his hand on the button. The rocket shudders for a moment then dies again. His action dislodges some of the rubbish covering the dashboard – and reveals a flashing button that has been hidden by the crisp packets and biscuit wrappers discarded by the boys, who seem to be almost permanently ravenous.

"Ah! The battery's flat," I say. "It needs charging."

"But it's been charging overnight!" Danny insists.

"Maybe it wasn't long enough after all those trips?" I suggest, which seems the most likely answer.

"Well, what do we do? We can't charge it now," Danny says, as if I'm the expert on rocket travel. I am sorely tempted to remind him that this entire fiasco is all his stupid idea but manage to refrain.

Outside, the wild sea creature rises up. A giant dragon-shaped head eyes us greedily and a long tongue snakes out and stabs at the rocket.

(NOTE - Look up dragons, firedrakes and wyverns.)

The rocket shoots backwards and Danny and

Modge fall off their seats as they aren't wearing their seatbelts as previously instructed. I ignore their cries and scan the manual for more information. It seems that I have to turn the wheel under my seat.

"What are you doing" Danny demands.

"The rocket can absorb power from the environment if I turn this wheel," I inform him. "Maybe the churning waves will give us enough of a charge."

(NOTE - Check the efficiency of wave power.)

The dragon snake comes again, this time with a wide open mouth, but a huge wave knocks us out of its way.

"Wave power will take ages!" Danny yells at me.

"Well what do you suggest, fart power? I don't think it will work, but you're both welcome to try!" I yell back because, honestly, I can't fix everything!

"You made a fart joke!" Danny says with a weird high-pitched laugh. "Ha ha ha! We might all be going to die but INAAYA made a fart joke! It's a miracle!"

(NOTE - It is NOT a miracle, merely the result of being surrounded by two idiots for days on end.)

I don't reply because the snake dragon finds us again and charges at us, its mouth wide enough to swallow us whole . . .

(NOTE - Look up how to survive being swallowed alive.)

Out of the dark and brooding sky a massive lightning strike hits the water. The lightning spreads across the surface of the water, the rocket hums as it absorbs the power, and when I slam my hand on the button one last time there is just enough energy to take us back home.

(NOTE - Now THAT, my friends, was an ACTUAL miracle!)

"Cleaning?" I ask Inaaya back at the IDLPO as she hands me a cloth and a bottle of Cif. "I didn't survive being eaten by an alien-monster-snake AND hit by lightning just to come back here and scrub toilets!"

"There's no point surviving if Echelon Xanadu shuts us down," Inaaya points out. "I was going to do the cleaning once we got back from all our trips but we have to wait for the rocket to recharge properly before we can take Shugly back, so we have to do the cleaning now. We can't leave any fresh traces of creatures downstairs, or he'll know your grandad's been breaking the rules."

I REALLY hate it when Inaaya's right.

I hate it even more when Inaaya's right about something that'll help me.

I take out my annoyance on the cages and scrub the last traces of creature presence from the pods and cages, while Inaaya mops the floor and Modge and Shugly polish the slightly singed rocket.

The thought of losing his new pet is clearly stressing Modge out, but I can't see any way round it. You wouldn't keep a lion in your garden, would you? Lions need to be running round the plains eating antelope. I know Modge understands really, but I'm still worried about how he'll cope without Shugly. He really does love him, and Shugly is definitely thriving under his care.

Finally Inaaya says we can finish so we go upstairs to get ready for our last trip. I go and grab the last of the snacks. Modge trails after me with Shugly snuggled in his hand.

"Do we really have to take him back, Danny?" he says. "Look how happy he is! He's grown lots since I got him and he just loves being with me. What if the other Fligglenogs are mean to him? What if there's no

one to scratch his chin?"

"He might have a family who are missing him though, Modge," I say.

"Or he might be an orphan?" Modge looks at me hopefully.

I sigh. This is going to be a really *loooong* day.

A blue light flashes and a minute later the office door slams opens. Echelon Xanadu storms in. I grab Modge and pull him down behind the desk with me before he can see us.

The inspector ploughs into the back room and I can hear Inaaya's startled squeak.

"You're early!" she says.

"I am PRECISELY on time. Forty-eight hours since I LEFT my office," he insists, possibly even beating Inaaya for smugness. "And ready to start inspecting."

"Bum bum bum bummity bum," I hiss because now what the flip are we supposed to do? We can't stay here. If Echelon finds Shugly, we're going to be in so much trouble! And worse than that, he'd be so massively annoyingly happy about it, I might explode.

"Where do you want to start?" Inaaya asks loudly.

"I think we'd best start in the creature containment

department," Echelon Xanadu says with glee. Almost as if he KNOWS we've been keeping creatures here, although of course that's impossible.

"Come on!" Modge says, tugging at my arm as soon as Inaaya and Echelon Xanadu go downstairs. He shuffles across the room to the outer door.

I have no choice but to follow him. "What are you doing?"

"Getting out of here. We can go through to your grandad's workshop and hide out there till he's gone," Modge says.

"We can't do that!" I say. "We're not allowed to take items out of the lost property office. What about that anomaly-whatsit thing Inaaya said?"

"I don't care! I'm not letting anyone send Shugly to the Hub!" Modge insists. "Besides, your grandad's office is empty. No one's going to see Shugly in there. It'll be fine."

"I don't know . . ." I bite my lip so hard it hurts.

"Danny, we have to go. There's no other way!"

"All right!" I grab my grandad's watch from my pocket, press it to the wall and five seconds later we stumble out into the cold and empty workshop.

A wave of longing for my grandad hits me. I miss him so much. I wish he was here fixing Mrs Atkins' toaster because she can't afford a new one, or mending an old bike he found in a skip for little Akim Chowdhary's birthday. I wish I was sitting next to him passing him screwdrivers and listening to his stories.

The silence in here is all wrong.

But the sudden suspicious burst of laughter coming from Grandad's office is even worse.

CHAPTER 19

I rush to the door, yank it open and see that poxy rat Keylon Molloy sitting in my grandad's chair with his feet up on my grandad's desk, munching through my grandad's biscuit tin, while his brother Sags types rude words on my grandad's typewriter. They're so busy they don't even notice me standing there.

"OY!" I yell as loud as I can.

Keylon and Sags jerk at my voice like electrocuted kippers. Keylon tips backwards out of the chair and lands on the floor. Sags leaps a foot in the air. They both get up and practically fall over each other, running to get out.

"Wait here," I order Modge.

Then I pelt after them, my blood boiling at their invasion. How DARE those lousy, stinky bum-heads break into my grandad's office! He's never done anything but good on this estate and this is how they repay him? I'll show them, I'll fight them both. Why not? I'm tough. I've seen *Rocky.* I can take on the Molloys. I'll teach them not to mess with me OR my grandad.

I'm so busy planning what I'm going to do to them when I catch them that I don't notice the skinny jean-clad leg sticking out of the side alley and go flying straight over it. I scrape all the skin off my hands when I land and crack my knee so hard it practically bounces off the concrete.

I roll around on the floor, hugging my leg and trying not to cry while Keylon emerges from the alley with a smug look on his face.

"You wanna look where you're going," Keylon says.

"And you two should stay out of my grandad's office!" I snap.

"No one tells the Molloys what to do!" Sags says, joining his brother.

Keylon bends down and picks something up off the floor.

"I mean it!" I tell them, trying to put a growl of menace in my voice. "Stay out of there!"

"Fine," Keylon says. "We'll just take this in

payment." He holds up my grandad's watch. It must have fallen out when I fell.

Panic wipes out the rest of my pain. I NEED that watch. Grandad trusted me to look after it, and without it Inaaya will be stuck in the IDLPO and me and Modge will be stuck out here on the estate with a creature from another dimension.

"You can't take that," I babble. "That's my grandad's watch."

Keylon shakes his head and grins at me. "No Danny, it's MY watch now."

"PLEASE, Keylon! You can't take it. I need it." I get to my feet and reach for the watch dangling from his hand, but Keylon shoves me away.

"I can do what I want, Danny!" he sneers. "This is OUR estate. No one messes with the Molloys!"

"EXCEPT ME!" Modge announces, bounding on to the scene like a really rubbish Avenger.

Keylon and Sags turn around, take one look at Modge with his hands on his hips, and start laughing. Sags stops first.

"Urgh!" Sags says, pointing at Modge. "What's that thing?"

I watch in horror as Shugly climbs out of Modge's
T-shirt and sits on his shoulder.

"Yeah, what is it?" Keylon demands, peering more
closely.

I feel dizzy with fear. I'm pretty sure showing weird
interdimensional creatures to people is enough to get
us executed, let alone locked up.

"Nothing," Modge says in a high-pitched squeak,
trying to grab Shugly from his shoulder.

"I've never seen nothing like it!" Sags says. "Get it,
Keylon! I always wanted a pet!"

The two brothers close in on Modge. Keylon
reaches out a hand to grab Shugly.

"GET OFF!" Modge bellows.

Shugly suddenly stands up on two legs and lets
out a sharp hiss. A frill of pale skin stands up around
his neck and sprays a burst of fine green liquid
straight into Keylon and Sags' faces. Sags and Keylon
cough, go still and then collapse unconscious on the
pavement.

Shugly's frill disappears and he starts licking his
paw like he didn't just murder two people.

I creep closer to the bodies. Thankfully their chests are rising and falling.

"Are they d . . . d . . . dead?" Modge stammers.

"No," I say, slightly giddy with relief. "But what the hell was that?"

Modge shrugs. "I dunno! He's never done it before. He must have got scared, you know, like when skunks spray that stinky stuff at predators?"

"Well, put him away before he sprays anyone else!"

"He didn't mean it," Modge says as he shoves Shugly back inside his shirt. "He was just trying to protect us."

I shake my head. "I don't think it matters. We're going to prison for this, Modge. Space prison. For a billion years."

"It was self-defence!" Modge says. "Besides, they had the key for the office! At least we can get it back now."

He's right about that, at least. I bend down to grab the watch from Keylon's hand.

As soon as I grab it, Keylon's eyes burst open and I stagger backwards into Modge. Sags wakes up too and they both look at me, confused and slightly more vacant than usual.

My brain spins trying to work out how we're going to explain ANY of this

"What happened?" Sags says, holding his head. "Why are we on the floor?"

"Wait . . ." Was this really possible? "You can't remember anything?" I double check.

"You were chasing us . . ." Keylon says. "That's the last thing I remember."

"Me too," groans Sags.

I glance at Modge. This is too good to be true. The

spray must have affected their memories which means that we've got away with it! No more prison! In fact this might be the perfect opportunity for some payback . . .

"Yeah . . . well, I caught you!" I tell the brothers with as much swagger as I can muster. "And I taught you both a lesson!"

"We BOTH did!" Modge adds.

"You did?" Keylon says, more confused than ever.

. "Yeah, we did!" I insist, looking him right in the eye. "So you better stay away from us and stay away from my grandad's office, or we'll finish what we started! Got it?"

Keylon and Sags nod slowly.

"Now get out of here!" I shout and the two brothers get up and run off.

"That was BRILLIANT!" Modge says, beaming at me.

"I know."

I sling my arm around his shoulders and we jump up and down a bit, united in this moment of long awaited triumph after years of being pushed around, before we remember we've left Inaaya alone in the IDLPO with Echelon Xanadu and we're risking interdimensional anomaly-whatsits by running around the estate with Shugly.

But still, it WAS totally epic.

"You should have seen Shugly, Inaaya!" Modge says, stroking Shugly's chin while the creature makes cute little rumbling noises. "He was amazing!"

Inaaya frowns. By the time we came back to the office Echelon was gone, but the whole thing had left Inaaya grumpy and fed up and not very impressed with tales of our triumph.

The inspection had gone well as Echelon hadn't found anything REALLY bad, but he'd been so annoyed that he'd discovered loads of small 'infractions' instead and listed them all on an official form. Really stupid things like:

Untidy paperclips – rule 78650001
Excessive biscuit crumbs – rule 99000000
Unlicensed tri-optical fish – rule 86765459

He made Inaaya promise to fix them all in the next thirty days or risk a penalty.

"Do you two realise what could have happened?" she says to us now. "You could have caused a cross-dimensional anomaly that destroyed the entire multiverse! You could have got caught with Shugly and accidentally revealed the truth about parallel dimensions!"

"Yeah, but –"

"But nothing! You were hugely irresponsible! You put us all at risk." Inaaya shakes her head. "Haven't you learned anything, Danny?"

A wave of shame washes over me. "It just . . . happened!" I try to explain.

"And Shugly was just trying to help!" Modge insists.

"We have to take him back. Right now," Inaaya says.

"What?" says Modge in horror. "Why? Echelon's gone, there's no rush any more."

"Yes, there is!" Inaaya insists. "He's dangerous. He can't stay here. Who knows what else he's capable of?"

"She's right," I tell Modge. "We have to take him back."

"But –"

"I'm sorry, Modge," His little face has crumpled up like an old paper bag. "I am. I know you love him but he

doesn't belong here. It's not fair to keep him, is it?"

"Yeah, but –"

"What if he has a family that's missing him?"

"But I'll miss him!" Modge wails.

"That's the job though, Modge," I say as gently as I can. "We help the creatures but we can't keep them."

Modge clutches Shugly to his chest and he looks so sad I can't bear it. I wish I could change things, make them better somehow, but I can't.

"Look, we can at least go and check out where he lives," I suggest, trying to make it easier for him. "His dimension might be amazing and then you'll be happy he has such a great home, won't you?"

"I suppose so." Modge sniffs. "And if it's terrible then he'll just have to come back with us."

"Let's discuss that when we get there," I say, crossing my fingers that Shugly lives in a rainbow paradise dimension somewhere.

Inaaya rolls her eyes at me. "So we're going then?"

"Just to see though," Modge says quickly.

"Right," Inaaya says. "Let's get it over with. I've got so much homework to do, it's ridiculous."

CHAPTER 20

"I don't like the look of it," Modge says the second we touch down in the Nog dimension.

"Oh, well, that's a surprise!" Inaaya says and I can't exactly blame her for doubting Modge's motives.

When I look out of the window though, I can see he's not exaggerating. It's pretty bleak here, a bit like our kitchen cupboards the day before Dad gets paid. There's nothing dangerous that I can see: no lava or flying rocks or exploding fruit. There's just an expanse of stone and dirt and sand. I can't see anything growing or anything living and the air is as dry and dusty as a tomb.

"We need to give it a proper chance, Modge," I tell him. "We should all get out and have a look round."

I press the door button and it slides open. "Come on."

I climb out of the rocket into the silent emptiness. Modge follows. It's so hot and dry I can almost feel my tongue shrivel up.

"And you should be prepared for Shugly to run off," Inaaya warns Modge as she joins us on the ground. "He's home now."

We move away from the rocket for a proper look around. Shugly sits inside Modge's shirt, his eyes turning this way and that. He makes no move to escape. If anything, he seems to sink deeper into his shirt nest.

"I don't think he likes it," Modge says.

"Give him a minute," I tell him because I'm not sure what happens now. We can't take him back, but can we really leave him here?

Inaaya bends down and picks up a handful of dirt. "It's almost like everything here died . . ." she says. "Even the earth."

"We'll have to take him back home," Modge says, trying not to sound too happy. "If we left him here, he'd probably die."

"But he can't live in the IDLPO forever, can he?" I say.

Modge grins. "Why not? Your grandad wouldn't mind."

"I suppose not," I admit. "But there are rules against it. We wouldn't be allowed to keep him."

"And Echelon is coming back in a month," Inaaya reminds us. "He'd find him and we'd all get arrested!"

"I'm not leaving him here!" Modge says. "He's my friend!"

"But we can't take him back!" Inaaya says.

The two of them look at me, both expecting me to side with them. I let out a huge sigh. Here we are again. These two arguing and me in the middle, and it's too much.

I just wish someone else would make the decision.

"We are more than happy to take him off your hands."

We spin round.

And find Kaspar and Kaylar Arachnus, looking just as shiny and creepy as always, standing next to their own very fancy and modern CAT.

I blink a few times to make sure I'm not seeing things. "What are you two doing here?" I gasp.

"We followed you, of course," says Kayla. "The

tracking device Echelon left on your vehicle made it easy."

"That twerp Echelon was working for you?" says Modge.

"Of course he was," Kaspar says. "We heard you mention a Fligglenog at the Hub and knew you were hiding something, so we found your location from the transporter records and sent him to poke around."

I knew that Echelon Xanadu was a rotten sneak! Of course he was working for the creepy Arachnus twins! The timing was too much of a coincidence.

"But why?" Inaaya asks because she needs to know EVERYTHING.

"For the creature, of course," Kaspar says slowly, like we're stupid. "We've been waiting a long time to find a Fligglenog and we weren't going to let this one get away. He's one of the reasons we set up the Hub in the first place."

"You're not doing this for the good of the creatures at all, are you?" I ask, but I already know the answer. My grandad was right to be suspicious!

Kaylar shrugs. "Of course not. It was a cover for finding the creatures we needed, that's all. This one is very rare. He might even be the last of his kind."

"You can't have him!" Modge says, backing away.

"Oh, now, don't be difficult," the siblings say in perfect harmony, walking towards Modge. "It's for the best. You children can't be in charge of something so special and we have great and important plans for him."

"I won't let you!" Modge insists, his eyes darting around wildly.

Kaspar and Kaylar close in and reach out to rip Shugly from Modge's T-shirt.

"NOW, SHUGLY!"

At Modge's yell, Shugly's frill comes up, the green spray hits Kaspar and Kaylar in the face and they immediately fall backwards on to the ground.

Inaaya gasps, a proper gasp of shock and awe, while me and Modge high-five each other.

"Told you it was cool!" I tell her.

"What do we do now though?" Modge says.

"Let's tie them up and take their keys," I suggest. "We can go and tell Mrs Arburknuckle what they did and –"

"Umm . . . Danny?" Inaaya says, her voice wavering.

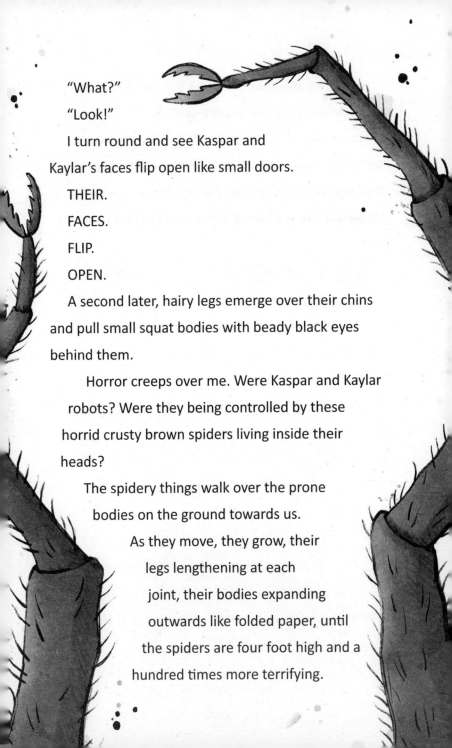

"What?"

"Look!"

I turn round and see Kaspar and Kaylar's faces flip open like small doors.

THEIR.

FACES.

FLIP.

OPEN.

A second later, hairy legs emerge over their chins and pull small squat bodies with beady black eyes behind them.

Horror creeps over me. Were Kaspar and Kaylar robots? Were they being controlled by these horrid crusty brown spiders living inside their heads?

The spidery things walk over the prone bodies on the ground towards us.

As they move, they grow, their legs lengthening at each joint, their bodies expanding outwards like folded paper, until the spiders are four foot high and a hundred times more terrifying.

I think Modge might faint he's gone so pale. Inaaya looks on the verge of screaming.

"Greetings," one of the spiders says in a low grating voice that scratches at my ears. "I am Z'os and this is Bee. We are from the Zonama dimension and we are taking over the multiverse."

CHAPTER 21

"B . . . b . . . but . . ." I stammer, fear and horror swamping my brain till it practically stops working.

"Your reaction does not surprise us. You are horrified by our appearance, are you not, human?" Z'os says. He's a bit bigger than the other creature but otherwise they look almost exactly the same. "Most citizens of the multiverse are. Despite the J'effians being one of the most advanced species of all the dimensions, we have faced terrible prejudice and abuse. A long time ago we realised we must hide our true forms and developed our 'skins'." One long leg points at the empty bodies of Kaspar and Kayla lying on the ground. "We based them on human bodies because they're harmless and unthreatening. Our skins make us acceptable to others and allow us to continue our work."

I swallow. "Your work?"

Z'os smiles. It's even more horrifying than when Kaspar does it. "Our plan to take over the multiverse. Centralus are incompetent fools, they don't deserve such power."

"How does building a creature Hub help you take over the multiverse?" Inaaya asks calmly but I can see she's trembling with fear.

"It was an easy way to get a foothold in Centralus," Bee says, lifting a thick scab from her skin with her pincers and dropping it into her mouth. I gag at the crunch as she chews it up, relishing the taste.

"Doing a good, charitable thing makes people trust us, like us, believe us," she continues. "Everyone loves creatures for some reason, so no one questions our motives. This allows us to harvest the creatures with certain abilities – like your Fligglenog here. We can weaponise all their powers and no one will EVER stand against the J'effians again!"

I get a flash of those poor creatures in the hidden room back at the Hub. That's why they had all those tubes and things stuck in them! These monsters were planning to use the lost creatures for their powers and didn't care what pain or misery they caused them!

Bee's beady eyes focus on Shugly.

Modge tries to run but it's too late. The spider shoots a silken rope from its fat body that winds around Modge like sticky string from waist to knees. Bee scrabbles towards him and snatches Shugly from beneath his T-shirt with the intricate boney pincers on her two front legs. Shugly struggles and squeaks – his ruff expands – but Z'os is ready with a pod and, before we can do anything, Shugly's already trapped inside.

Modge struggles in his sticky cage but can't escape. "Stop it! Give him back!" he cries, furious tears in his eyes.

Z'os and Bee ignore him.

"This creature produces an excellent mind serum in two glands in its neck," says Z'os. "We shall keep it caged, drain its serum and use it to ensure no one learns anything they shouldn't. It was one of our main prizes, but we have others. Each one will help us in our plans."

"So you lied to all the caretakers?" Inaaya says. The truth about the Arachnus billionaires is hitting her hard, I think.

Bee laughs, only it sounds more like a frog croaking. "Of course we lied. We don't care about the creatures!"

"But you were helping them get home!" Inaaya says, trying to claw some good out of the situation.

Z'os shrugs. "Well, we sent most of them back. How many actually survived the trip is unknown. The stress of travel via transporter is probably too extreme for some."

Modge erupts, swearing furiously and straining at

his bonds but Z'os just laughs and shoots a webbing ball which splats over Modge's mouth like a seal, muffling his words.

Inaaya clenches her fists. "I suppose you were lying about your plans for the lost property as well?"

"Of course!" says Z'os. "Taking over the lost property is the next stage of our plan. Imagine how many useful objects are lying around, just waiting to be discovered."

I think of the pencil-laser-blaster-matter-dematerialiser we found on day one. How many other terrible weapons or dangerous artefacts might be lying in a lost property office somewhere?

Bee continues. "Between the lost creatures and the lost property, we should have everything we need to launch our assault on Centralus headquarters and take over their entire operation."

"And what will you do for the multiverse that's so amazing?" I demand.

Bee and Z'os do that creepy thing where they speak at the same time. "We will turn it into the very first interdimensional shopping destination!"

I'm sure my jaw hits the floor. Shopping? This

entire terrible, evil plan is over shopping?

"We can sell the lost property and the lost creatures that have no value to us across the multiverse and deliver it all in seconds using our transporter," says Bee gleefully. "It's pure profit. We don't have to pay for any of the stock but we can sell it at any price we choose!"

"But that property belongs to other people!" I shout, remembering all the toys I'd lost that Grandad had brought back for me, all the purses and keys and memories that we boxed up and sent into storage.

Z'os laughs. "They lost it! Why should the multiverse pay Centralus taxes to fund a system of returns when people are careless enough to lose their own things in the first place? Anyway. Enough chat. We have what we came for . . ."

Bee and Z'os scuttle back towards their CAT, taking Shugly with them.

"Wait!" Inaaya calls, worry and panic laced into her voice. "You can't do this Don't you know there's a risk of interdimensional anomalies when you send items between the dimensions? It's far too dangerous!"

Z'os shakes his head. "The risk is minuscule!

Centralus uses that threat as a way to control the dimensions, ensuring many are kept technologically inferior to others. We are allowing every dimension to be part of our enterprise. If they can afford to buy it, they can have it."

"But you're massively increasing the odds of an anomaly happening!" Inaaya insists. "Each time you sell something and send it to another dimension, the odds will get higher. Eventually you could bring down the entire multiverse!"

Z'os shrugs. "That could take millenia. Why worry about it now?"

"You'd risk destroying the entire multiverse just for profit?" I ask because I don't understand. They live here too! Why would they destroy the world just for money when they're already super rich?

"What is life without risk?" Bee says as if that makes sense.

"We won't let you do this! We'll warn everyone!" Inaaya shouts.

Modge tries to agree, nodding his head, his eyes huge and desperate.

"That might be difficult if you never return," says Z'os.

He points an arm at our CAT and sends a ball of web at the engine, smashing a hole straight through it and destroying our only chance of ever returning home.

"You're just going to leave us here?" I gasp, panic clawing at my chest and making it hard to breathe.

I don't want to DIE out here!

I don't want to die AT ALL!

"It's all right. You won't last very long," Bee tells us. "The Nog Dimension is basically dead, we drained everything useful from it decades ago. Nothing grows here any more and it's all crumbling to dust. That's why this Fligglenog is so important. His egg was probably left here long ago and only hatched recently due to temperature fluctuations. It was a miracle he fell through the wyrm hole before he died."

"You can't do this!" I shout, even though I already know they will. There's nothing in those black eyes when they look at us, except cold, hard calculation.

"Of course we can, foolish human!" says Bee. "Your tragic loss while performing your duties will help us persuade Centralus to sign the contract giving us full power over ALL the IDLPOs. Once we have access to the Centralus mainframe multiverse codes, nothing will be able to stop us."

"Someone else will figure it out!" says Inaaya.

Z'os tips his brown head to one side, considering.

"Perhaps. But IF they do, we now have the perfect serum to help them forget whatever they've seen or heard."

Inaaya glares at them like a furious avenging angel. "You're both monsters! Killing children just to cover up your evil plans!"

"The multiverse has treated US like monsters for millennia," Z'os says, a cold fury shining in his black eyes. "The simple truth is our species has no time for useless sentiment or empathy. We crave profit and power. And soon we will be the richest, most powerful monsters in the multiverse and nothing will be able to stop us. Certainly not you three imbeciles!"

The Je'ffians turn away from us. Z'os drags their human 'skins' behind them to their CAT. Modge struggles and moans as Bee climbs in and Shugly disappears from view. Within seconds they're gone, leaving us alone and stranded in a dying dimension.

CHAPTER 22

Inaaya rushes to look at the damage to our CAT.

"It's destroyed," she groans. "Totally destroyed. There's no way to fix it."

"Can you bring me a screwdriver or something?" I ask her, trying to free Modge from the web wrapped around him. "This web is really tough."

Inaaya crosses the dusty, arid ground and shoves my grandad's trusty multi tool in my hand. "Did you hear me? Those evil spider twins have gone and the three of us are stuck here for good!"

I use the sharp knife to cut through the web until Modge is finally free and peel the seal away from his mouth, before tucking the multi tool in my pocket.

"I can't believe those scummy spiders took my Shugly!" Modge says, rubbing at his eyes.

Inaaya lets out a growl of frustration. "Your ridiculous obsession with that creature is what got us here in the first place!"

"Oh, I'm sorry for caring about creatures and helping to uncover a terrible plot that could destroy the multiverse!" Modge growls back. "I suppose you'd have just let them get away with it?"

"They ARE getting away with it!" Inaaya shouts back. "We can't stop them if we're stuck here, can we? So now we're just going to die out here in this miserable desert for NOTHING!"

"Well, you're the one who kept saying how amazing those two were," Modge snaps. "How generous and wonderful they were. I'M the one who said they couldn't be trusted. But you never listen to me, do you? You think you're so clever and special, always looking down on us and bossing us about, but you can't even tell who the real monsters are!"

I stare at Modge in shock. He's always been so laid back, but right now he looks angry enough to explode.

Inaaya starts pacing in a circle. "Excuse me for not knowing there were massive spiders living inside two people! Excuse me for helping you two out of all the trouble you keep getting into, even though you NEVER say thank you and treat me like your bossy, annoying older sister. Do you think I want to do all the work while you two just mess about?"

"Yeah, I do actually," Modge hisses. "You love showing off and lording it over us! Why else would you help us?"

My head is thumping, my guts are churning and these two just won't shut up.

"ENOUGH!" I yell. "I'm so sick of you two arguing. You both got us into this mess with your constant fighting. You were supposed to be helping me, but you messed everything up instead!"

Inaaya stops pacing and they both turn and glare at me.

"What?" I say. "It's true!"

"Not everything is about you!" Inaaya says furiously. "We've both gone out of our way to help you and you've never even once said thank you! Do you even know how much trouble I'm in at school?"

I tut loudly. "You and your precious school! I'm sorry you're late with your stupid homework, all right?"

"No, it's not all right actually! I have to keep up my grades or I'll lose my scholarship."

I roll my eyes. "Boo hoo hoo."

"Oh, shut up!" Inaaya yells, stamping her foot in fury. "My parents could never afford to send me to that school, Danny. They can't even afford anywhere to live!"

"What?" Now I'm really confused. "What do you mean?"

"You are so dim!" Inaaya shouts. "That day we came to visit you was so my mum could ask if we could come and stay at yours."

"But . . . why?" I mean, they've got a perfectly

good house with four bedrooms and a big garden with a tree house in the back.

Inaaya's shoulders sag and she suddenly looks exhausted. "Because my dad lost his job, didn't he?" she says. "And then he couldn't pay the mortgage and the bank repossessed our house – that's why. Me and Mum came to stay at yours so I could keep going to school, and my dad took my brother to Birmingham to stay with his uncle and work in his shop."

It takes me a minute to catch up. "So . . . when my grandad had a heart attack . . ."

" . . . we'd already arranged to come and stay."

I feel like an idiot. Poor Inaaya. I feel rotten now. It must be rubbish to have nowhere to live and your family all split up, and I've just been making her help me all the time. I realise that I've been so worried about all the lost property stuff that I hadn't given anyone else a thought. Hadn't even really noticed how stressed Aunt Rekha was, even though it was pretty obvious the way she was cleaning and cooking every minute of the day.

"I'm sorry, Inaaya. I didn't know," I say.

Inaaya sighs. "I know. Mum didn't want you to. She's really embarrassed about it all."

"It's not your fault though."

"I know but she is anyway." My cousin chews at her plait. "All she talks about now is me doing well at school and becoming a doctor or a dentist or something, so she can be proud of me and have something to boast about."

"I thought you wanted to be an astrophysicist though?" I say.

"I do," Inaaya says. "But I might not get any choice. I need to make my parents proud, Danny, especially now. If I lose my place at school, Mum will be devastated."

I feel worse than ever. "I didn't know Inaaya, not any of it."

"Yeah, well, you don't notice anything except your own stuff, do you?" She shakes her head at me like I'm a lost cause. "You don't even know why your best friend has been acting like a deranged mother troll, all over some little pet!"

"I was just waiting for him to tell me why when he was ready, actually!" I snap back, feeling really angry all of a sudden. Of course I knew something else was wrong! Modge has been my best mate for YEARS.

don't need Inaaya to tell me.

I look at my friend but he won't catch my eye.

"Modge?"

I get a weird prickly feeling in my belly. Maybe I should have pushed him a bit more. I thought it was something small bothering him, something easy to fix, but what if it's actually something really bad?

"What is it, Modge?" I press. "You can tell me."

Modge sniffs and scuffs his shoes in the dirt. "I just wanted Shugly to have someone to love him," he mutters. "Someone who would never leave him, no matter what, because it's horrible when that happens, Danny. Really horrible."

"Yeah," I say carefully. "I can see that."

He does a big sigh, then blurts out, "And when I saw my mum last time she told me she was getting married and moving to Scotland and she wants me to go and live with her."

My whole belly plummets. "What? Why didn't you tell me?"

He shrugs. "Cos if I told you then it would make it real."

"So . . . are you going?" I ask, feeling sick at the

thought of losing him.

"I dunno. Mum really wants me to go."

"What about your dad?"

"He says it's up to me."

"And?"

Modge makes a long huffing noise. "I dunno! I missed my mum for years. I always used to imagine her coming back to get me and us living together and how great it would be, but now I'm not sure."

"Right." I rub my hands over my face, feeling awful for letting Modge struggle with all of this on his own. Of course he wants to live with his mum. My mum's only been gone a few days and I miss her like mad. This is the perfect opportunity for Modge to make up for all the years she's been out of his life.

Modge looks at me. "I am sorry, Danny. I should have told you. It was just easier to ignore it all."

"No, I'M sorry," I say honestly. "I knew there was something wrong. I should have taken the time to find out what it was."

"You've been a bit busy."

"Busy messing things up as usual," I mutter.

"It's not your fault!" Modge says because he's just

too nice for his own good. I don't deserve him. I don't deserve either of them.

I look at Modge and Inaaya, stuck out here in the middle of the multiverse with no way home, just because they were trying to help me, and feel like the biggest loser in the world.

"I'm so sorry, about everything, all of this," I burst out. "I was so obsessed with my own stuff I forgot to be a good friend. You've both helped me out loads and I never even said thank you. All of this is my fault."

"I think you'll find it's actually the rotten spider monsters' fault," Inaaya says with a small smile.

"Doesn't matter whose fault it is, I suppose." I slump down on a flattish rock. The reality of our situation is finally sinking in. "We're still going to die here and those spider faces are going to turn the multiverse into a ginormous poxy shopping mall that might explode at any minute."

Inaaya snorts and Modge laughs and I can't help joining them. What else can we do? It's all so stupid. We laugh and laugh till our stomachs hurt.

"Oh well. At least I don't have to worry about my

homework any more!" Inaaya says, flopping down next to me.

"And I guess I won't be living with either of my parents, seeing as I'll be dead!" Modge adds, nudging his bum on to the rock beside me.

"And my grandad's already out of a job thanks to the spider faces," I say, "so he can't blame me!"

"Guess everything's just fine then!" Inaaya says.

"Yup," I agree, even though nothing is fine at all, however much we pretend.

We plunge into silence, the dust of a dying dimension blowing restlessly about our feet.

CHAPTER 23

After a while Modge says he's hungry and heads to the broken CAT to forage for snacks.

"They'll start missing us soon," Inaaya says.

"Yeah." I'd been complaining about Aunt Rekha's feasts but I wish I was there now, scooping up curry with my chapati and listening to my dad talk about cricket. I wonder when he'll phone my mum and tell her. She'll have to tell my grandad, I suppose.

I've been missing them both so much, but this is worse than ever. Before I knew I'd see them again, eventually. Now . . .

"There's two packets of Monster Munch, a Curly Wurly and a Twix," Modge says, dumping a plastic bag at my feet. "I ate the Mars bar already on the way back. Sorry."

I nod.

"We should ration them, I suppose," Inaaya says, eyeing the small pile of snacks. "There might not be much other food here."

"Much food? I don't think there's ANY food! Or water! Or shelter! I mean, look at this place!" I wave my arms at the desolate landscape.

"There might be something," Inaaya says. "We should check at least."

"Why?" I say. "So we can live a few extra miserable days or weeks?"

"Maybe someone will rescue us," Modge says.

"Who?" I ask. "No one knows where we are except the poop heads who left us here in the first place."

"Shugly knows."

"Yeah, and they're going to keep him in a cage draining his brain serum!"

Modge gulps.

Inaaya glares at me. "I'm sure they'll look after him, Modge. They need him so they have to make sure he's all right, don't they?"

"Poor Shugly," Modge says. "First he hatches in this terrible place, then he falls through a wyrm hole and ends up stolen by evil spider faces."

"He had a good time when he was with you though, Modge," I remind him. "You looked after him. Remember how epic it was when he sprayed the Molloys?"

Modge smiles. "So epic!"

"He loved being with you," Inaaya says.

"Yeah. He was probably a bit lonely here, all alone. It was lucky he fell through the wyrm hole at all really."

'Wait . . ." I say as something clicks in my head.

"What?"

"Shugly fell through a wyrm hole."

"We know that!"

"Ssssshhh." My brain whirrs for a second. "The computer gave us the coordinates of where he was last. And that's where the CAT brought us."

"So?"

I stand up, start pacing. "So that means there must be a wyrm hole round here somewhere. If we find it, we can go through it and back to our IDLPO! Right, Inaaya?"

Inaaya stares at me. I grin back. We don't have to die. We can go home. Back to our estate, back to our lives.

"Danny's right," she says slowly. "I mean there's no guarantee it will take us back to OUR IDLPO, but we should be able to get home again from there."

"So we can go home?" Modge says.

"If we can find the wyrm hole."

"Let's start looking then!"

"There's only one problem," I tell him. "How do you look for a wyrm hole when you don't know what they look like?"

"You can't look for them," Inaaya says. "They're invisible. That's how creatures fall through them. Why no one notices them."

I sag. Obviously it was too good to be true.

"But there might be a way . . ." she says slowly. "Remember the disturbance of the wyrm hole at the office made our phones stop working?"

"Yeah."

"Well, maybe we can use our phones as detectors?" she says. "Mine's working now – well, it's on anyway. I can't exactly call anyone, but if we walk around with our phones we can see when they stop working and that might help us find the wyrm hole."

I take a deep breath. "Inaaya, have I ever told you

you're a flipping genius?"

She smiles at me. "Not as often as you should have, clearly. But you're the one who came up with this brilliant idea, Danny."

I shrug modestly, secretly pleased with her praise. "I only got the idea because of what Modge said."

Modge isn't listening, though. He's halfway through a packet of pickled onion Monster Munch.

"What?" he says when he sees us looking at him, crumbs spraying from his mouth. "I'll need lots of energy to look for an invisible wyrm hole, won't I?"

I mean, I'm really glad we ended up back at our own IDLPO, but we REALLY should have thought it through. Maybe then we wouldn't all be squashed together now, inside the blue net with all the other lost items, totally unable to move.

Even though it took us HOURS and HOURS to find the wyrm hole Shugly fell through, we didn't ever consider what might happen to us when we did. To be fair, we were all starving and thirsty and tired after

traipsing around the Nog dimension for ages and starting to worry we'd be stuck there forever. Or until we died a long agonising death anyway.

And then, when it finally happened, it was so quick there was no time to plan anything. One minute Modge was there and then he wasn't. I heard him squeak, looked up and he was gone. I yelled for Inaaya, ran over to the scrubby bit of bush where Modge had been standing and then WHOOSH, I was sucked down into a vortex. I imagine it's a similar feeling to being flushed down a toilet, except not as wet, just whirling round and round and round till you can't remember who you are, let alone where you're going.

After about a million years of this the whirling eventually stopped. There was a split second of relief when I saw that Modge and Inaaya had showed up. But now we're all squashed together like sardines in a can, except not quite as smelly.

We can't talk, which might be just as well – and we can't move – which is a disaster because:

Inaaya's elbow is digging into my ribs.

Modge's bum is pressed WAY too close against my face.

I really need to do a wee and we can't pull the lever and escape the blue net trapping us, so we're basically stuck in here forever.

I'm just imagining the horrible picture of Mrs Arburknuckle turning up in a week or so to find us all floating about in a yellow cloud of my wee when the alarm starts going off.

A small box falls into the net, taking up the last inch of available space.

The alarm goes into overdrive.

"WARNING! MAXIMUM CAPACITY REACHED. MAXIMUM CAPACITY REACHED."

Oh great. How flipping marvellous to see things are getting EVEN better.

What the hell do we do now?

What exactly happens when the net is too full and there's no one to empty it?

Sparks sizzle across the net and then it slowly breaks apart. The contents spill to the floor and me and Modge and Inaaya are dumped in a pile, among rainbow-coloured elf pants, talking pebbles and several spiky flurble hats.

CHAPTER 24

I take a minute to recover and enjoy the use of my body again before shouting "SHUT UP!" at the alarm. It thankfully does as it's told, bringing a welcome silence to the office.

"I can't believe we broke the net!" Inaaya says, getting to her feet. "We are going to be in so much trouble!"

"Who cares about the net?" I ask her. "We're back in our dimension! We're not going to die in stupid awful Nog! Be happy!"

"I'll be happy when we get Shugly back," Modge says.

"And I'll be happy once we've stopped those awful spider faces!" Inaaya adds.

"Yeah, well I'll be happy once I've had a wee!" I tell them before running off to the toilet.

When I get back, Modge and Inaaya are raiding the biscuit tin and opening cans of drink. I join them sharpish before it's all gone, and for a long while the only noise is of chomping and gurgling as we try and refill our bellies.

Eventually only crumbs and crushed cans remain and I'm feeling slightly more normal.

"What day is it?" I ask because I'm so tired I can't remember any more.

"Still Sunday?" says Modge. "I think?"

"When are the Centralus delegation having the meeting at the Hub?"

Inaaya checks her wrist watch. "In about an hour!"

"Okay then," I take a deep breath and flex my biceps. "Let's get over to the Hub, save the day and get back home before our parents discover we've been lying to them."

"Good plan!" Modge says.

"It would be," Inaaya says. "Except how are we going to get to the Hub? We don't have the CAT any more so we can't fly there. And we don't have any creatures so the beam won't come and take us."

I groan loudly. I can't believe there's ANOTHER

problem. This stuff never flipping happens to real superheroes.

"But . . . we have to get there! We need to rescue Shugly!" Modge says, his lower lip trembling.

"We didn't survive all that just so we can fail now," I insist. "We have to think of something."

"We could wait for a creature to come through the net?" Inaaya says.

"But that could take days, or weeks!" Modge says, chewing at his nails.

"Can we trick the scanner? Use something else, like old fur from the last creature we took back or something?" I ask.

"Danny, it's a highly sensitive bit of equipment," says Inaaya. "I don't think using a bit of grotty old fur is going to work. And anyway, we cleaned out all the cages, remember?"

I groan. I knew all that cleaning was a bad idea. What are we going to do now? If we don't stop Z'os and Bee then Centralus will sign a contract with those scum spiders and we'll never stop them! They'll end up destroying the entire multiverse unless we reveal the truth about their evil arachnid plans.

"What about an egg?" Modge says.

"An egg?" Inaaya frowns. "What sort of egg?"

"A Shugly egg?" Modge suggests, holding out a small silvery ball.

Inaaya's eyes widen. "Where did you get that?"

"I picked it up in the Nog dimension when we were looking for the wyrm hole," he says. "There were a few of them together and one of them was broken into pieces, like something had hatched out of it, and the others were kind of squashed and black but this one looked perfect.

I just thought Shugly might like a brother or sister, so I picked it up."

Inaaya peers closely at it.

"It might just be a weird rock . . ."

"But we should put it in the scanner," I say. "Just in case."

"We should," Inaaya says. "We should also put all the lost property somewhere safe.

Hopefully they can fix the net later."

We spend five minutes scooping up jars of ogre wart powder and fairy flower dresses and throwing them into the sorting hole.

"Is that everything?" Inaaya asks.

"Yep," Modge says.

"Ready to go?"

I nod and yawn at the same time. All this saving the multiverse is EXHAUSTING. I press the button on the lever and the whadjamacallit rises up.

"Go on then, Modge," I say. "Put it on the conveyor belt and if it's an egg we have to be ready to grab hold when the transport ray comes, okay?"

"Okay."

Fingers crossed.

We all watch the silver ball travel along the conveyor belt, heading towards the scanner.

```
Fligglenog egg from Dimension NOG
HIGHLY RARE
Interdimensional transport to
Centralus Hub activated.
```

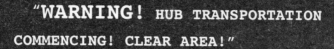

"**WARNING!** HUB TRANSPORTATION COMMENCING! CLEAR AREA!"

"You did it, Modge!" I slap him on the back and he beams at me.

"Get ready, everyone!" Inaaya says.

She grabs the label and sticks it on the egg and the blue ray comes down. Modge holds the egg, Inaaya holds Modge, I grab hold of them both – and we're sucked back through the transporter to the Hub.

I had hoped that being prepared might make the journey easier, but nope. It still feels like I've been in the washing machine for a week.

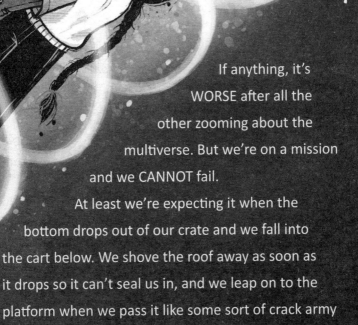

If anything, it's
WORSE after all the
other zooming about the
multiverse. But we're on a mission
and we CANNOT fail.

At least we're expecting it when the
bottom drops out of our crate and we fall into
the cart below. We shove the roof away as soon as
it drops so it can't seal us in, and we leap on to the
platform when we pass it like some sort of crack army
troop.

"Right, let's find out where the meeting is!"
Inaaya says.

"We need to find Shugly first!" Modge says, slipping the egg that got us here into his pocket.

"Why? He's fine. We can rescue him after. It's more important to stop the meeting, Modge!"

"They've got him hooked up to a DRAIN, Inaaya!"

Arguing. More arguing. I feel like screaming, but that might not be a great idea on a secret mission against monstrous spider-creatures, so I let out a long groan instead.

"What do you think, Danny?" Modge and Inaaya say at the same time, staring at me, willing me to choose their suggestion.

But what if I get it wrong? I don't want the fate of the multiverse resting on my shoulders. I'm not clever enough, not good enough, not responsible enough. My grandad should never have left me in charge. How am I supposed to know what to do?

I really wish my grandad was here now. He'd do the right thing. He always did the right thing, that's why I trusted him so much. I knew he'd never let me down. He'd never let anyone down.

A cog turns slowly in my brain.

If I really DO trust him, then I have to believe he

did the right thing making me caretaker.

I close my eyes and remember him lying on the floor in the workshop, pressing his precious watch into my hands. Trusting ME to look after everything he loved most.

So, really, the problem isn't whether he trusted me, but that I don't trust myself.

If I thought about it, I had done whatever was necessary to keep the IDLPO running so far. I'd even gone to Inaaya for help when I REALLY didn't want to and that was a good decision – not that I'd ever tell her that, obviously . . . well, maybe I would if it was her birthday, or something.

I let Modge bring Shugly back to the IDLPO, even though it was breaking the rules, because I could sense there was something wrong at the Hub and I was right about that too.

I'd travelled across the multiverse returning creatures to their homes because I believed it was the right thing to do and it TOTALLY was. And somehow, all of those things led to us uncovering a dangerous plot to destroy the multiverse. And THEN, when we were nearly foiled by the bad guys and facing death, I was the one who figured out a way for us to get back home.

I open my eyes and set my shoulders back. It's time for me to take charge. I can do this.

"We're going to get Shugly." I hold my hand up to stop Inaaya's protests. "We know where they're keeping him AND we can find out what other rare creatures they have with him, just in case they're planning to use any of them during the meeting."

Inaaya sniffs. "I suppose that makes sense."

"Good. Let's go then. And this time, let's not get caught immediately."

"Let's not get caught at all!" Inaaya adds.

And I've never agreed with her more. We have to do this properly because everything – literally EVERYTHING – depends on us.

CHAPTER 25

The Hub is entirely deserted and we find the infirmary easily. It looks like before, clean and shiny with a few healthy-looking creatures in pods just for show.

I lead Modge and Inaaya down to the secret room, but as we approach I can hear a voice through the open door.

". . . Just a little bit more, that's it, well done."

I peer round the corner and see the vet we met on our tour bending over one of the pods.

"It's Dr Triffle Iffle. Let's just wait till he's gone," I whisper to Modge and Inaaya.

Modge barges straight past me and storms into the room like an enraged mother bear, scanning the pods.

"WHAT HAVE YOU DONE WITH MY SHUGLY?" he shouts.

"Er . . . what are you three

younglings doing here? This is a top secret restricted area!" the vet squeaks.

"How can you work for those monsters?" Inaaya demands, following Modge inside. "You're a vet! You're supposed to care about creatures."

"Kaspar and Kaylar are doing wonderful work!" the vet protests, looking nervous.

"Not them," says Inaaya. "The monsters living inside them."

Dr Triffle Iffle staggers backwards in shock. "You know about that?"

"They tried to kill us!" I say.

"Oh, you can't imagine how awful it's been!" he cries, almost sobbing. "I have been doing my best, yes indeed, to care for the poor creatures, but I knew there was something terrible going on!"

"WHERE'S SHUGLY?" Modge demands again.

"Who?"

"The Fligglenog," Inaaya explains.

"Oh, here he is. Poor thing." Dr Triffleiffle picks up the round plastic pod behind him. "They drained his glands and it left him quite ill. He's been miserable."

Modge pounces on the pod, rips it open and

snatches up his friend. There are two damp patches on the fur around Shugly's neck.

Modge sits on the floor and carefully cradles Shugly in his arms.

After a minute, Shugly lifts his head and makes a soft mewling sound and Modge kisses him carefully on the nose.

I turn back to the vet. "You knew what they were up to but you did nothing to stop them?"

"I wanted to but they have my family," the vet says quietly, shaking his froggy head. "My four wifelings and my nineteen sproglets. How could I put them at risk? Besides, who would ever have believed me? The J'effians have been long believed extinct. Who could imagine they were living inside fake bodies all this time and plotting to take over the multiverse?"

"How did you find out about them?" Inaaya asks.

"An unlucky accident. Kaylar was hit by a Freeziflea during testing – her skin froze up so she opened the face and climbed out. Unsurprisingly, I fainted from the shock. When I came round they were both back in their skins and staring at me. They told me it was all a dream but I knew it wasn't. That's when they took my family."

"What's a Freeziflea?" says Modge, looking interested.

"They live on the CristalSnurt." Dr Triffle Iffle points to another pod, holding a beautiful frosted white creature with nine blue eyes and a vicious set of fangs. "The fleas drink the CristalSnurt's near-frozen blood, and when they're thrown, they explode and their insides freeze whatever they hit for a few minutes."

I gulp. "Wow. I guess that's another one of their weapons then."

"You have it there, exactly. They've already packaged them up, look!" The vet shows us a row of tubes packed with pea-sized Freezifleas on a higher shelf. "And they've already found a way to concentrate the essence from the Fligglenog so it lasts far longer than normal. They are a remarkably clever species, but they have no scruples. I am afraid they will not stop until they have taken control of everything and turned the multiverse into an empty wasteland." Dr Triffle Iffle rubs his paws together nervously.

"Do you know what they're planning?" I ask.

The vet shakes his head. "I do not. They're very excited about the meeting though. The Centralus delegation should be arriving here any minute."

"We have to stop them signing the contract and getting access to the mainframe codes," Inaaya says. "If they get their way they'll turn the multiverse into a giant shop, selling off creatures and lost property and anything else they can."

"Cross-dimensional shopping? My goodness!" The vet looks like he might faint. "That's been banned for centuries because of the risks."

"They don't care about the risks," Inaaya tells him. "They don't care about anything except profit."

The vet shakes his head. "I find myself unsurprised. The J'effian race have a long history of most dangerous dealings. That is why they were banned from trading and ostracised by most dimensions in the multiverse."

"They told us they were judged because of how they looked," Inaaya says.

"They cried discrimination but it was never that," the doctor says. "They will take and take and take until there is nothing left. They destroyed entire species, entire ecosystems. They didn't care, just moved on to the next. Destroying for profit is all they do."

"Couldn't you have told someone what was happening, done something to stop them?" I ask.

"My family," he reminds us quietly. "The risk to my family was too great when there was no way of proving my words."

"Well, we're not going to let them do this!" I tell him. "That's why we're here."

"Do you have a plan, younglings?"

Did we have a plan? Did we have a plan?

No. Of course we didn't have a poxy plan.

CHAPTER 26

I look at Modge cuddling Shugly. The little creature is
making soft purring noises now and looks half asleep.

"They're monsters, that's what they are!" Modge
fumes. "How can they treat poor, defenceless
creatures like this?"

The vet shrugs. "The J'effians don't care at all for
another living thing. If Centralus sign that contract
and give them the access codes for the mainframe
we've got no chance."

"We'll tell them the truth about the J'effians!" says
Modge.

"Centralus would never believe us, not without
proof," I say.

"We could give Centralus proof.
Force the creepy twins to leave
their skins with one of those

Freeziflea things?" Modge suggests.

"Way too dangerous! I never want to set eyes on those spider monsters again," Inaaya says with a shudder "No, it's safest to just convince the delegation not to sign. Then after we've all left the Hub we can tell them the truth, Dr Triffle Iffle will back us up won't you?"

The vet trembles.

"Centralus will come and deal with them and they'll find your family," Inaaya says and the vet takes a big, slightly snotty, breath and then nods.

"But how do we convince the delegation not to sign?" Modge argues.

"By being honest," I tell them slowly.

"Isn't that the same as Modge's plan about being truthful?" Inaaya says.

"Not quite," I say. My mind is whirring with an idea that might just be possible if we all work together.

"The meeting is starting in a few minutes, so you should probably hurry over there if you want to stop them," Dr Triffle Iffle says.

"Okay," I say. "We're just going to need your help with a few things first . . ."

The promotional slideshow is coming to an end at last. Dr Triffle Iffle had let us into the control room earlier and from here we can see everything that's happening in the meeting room.

The Centralus delegates are all seated in front of the screen, they include one very large spotty snail wearing a furry hat, a stalk eyed gentlemen with large gossamer wings and antennae, a smart green woman with hooves for feet, a tiny man with a HUGE moustache riding a caterpillar and our very own Mrs Arburknuckle. They're all fidgeting and looking restless after nearly an hour of statistics and general showing off from Kaspar and Kaylar.

"Are you ready?" I ask Inaaya.

"Nearly." Her fingers fly over the keyboard as she puts the finishing touches into the computer that runs the entire Hub.

"Thank you all for your attention," Kaspar says as the screen goes dark. "I hope you can now all see how valuable the Hub is, and are ready to sign the contract enabling us to work with all the IDLPOs."

"Inaaya! We have to do it now!" I tell her, my gaze fixed on the four large video screens that allow us to zoom in and out on events.

Inaaya swivels in her chair and presses one final button. "Okay. It's ready."

The screen in the meeting room lights up suddenly with the words "THE TRUTH ABOUT THE HUB."

"The slideshow you just saw does not show the truth about what happens at the hub," Inaaya's voice comes through the speakers loud and clear in the meeting room as video footage of the creature coaster stolen from the security footage begins to play.

Kaylar immediately leaps in front of the screen to

try and block the view. "We seem to be having some technical difficulties," she says as her brother tries to turn the slideshow off by jabbing his fingers at the buttons. He won't be able to though. Inaaya's routed everything through to the control room.

"And as if this barbaric creature coaster wasn't bad enough," Inaaya's voice says into the microphone, "these poor scared creatures are then forced to endure this invasive and extremely stressful procedure."

The video shows the beetles being poured into the carts.

"If you could please all leave the room while we fix this . . ." Kaspar says loudly, trying to herd the delegation outside.

"They can't leave! They need to keep watching!" I shout at the video screen.

"Actually, I'd like to see this," Mrs Arburknuckle says with all the firmness of a grumpy PE teacher on a rainy sports day. "ALL OF IT."

"Ha! Mrs A is such a legend," I say.

"Do you think it's working?" Modge asks, hugging Shugly close.

"It will," Inaaya says. "Just give it a chance."

The delegation watch a close-up of the sad creatures in the carts with the hordes of beetles crawling all over them. Their low murmurings are upset and angry, and exactly what we were hoping to achieve.

"And the brilliant healthcare on offer?" Inaaya's voice says as video footage of the secret room comes up, innocent creatures attached to tubes and drains. "This is what it really looks like."

"It's working!" I say, seeing shock and horror fill the room. "Look at the delegates' faces!"

Best of all though, Kaspar and Kaylar's rage has twisted their perfect features into snarling beasts.

But there's nothing they can do. Not if they want the delegation to sign.

"Ooh! Time for our greatest weapon!" Inaaya says as the video I made earlier of Modge and Shugly starts to play in the meeting room.

She pulls the microphone closer. "This baby Fligglenog comes from a drained and desolate dimension," Inaaya's David Attenborough impression is a bit much but the delegates are drinking it up. "It might be the very last of his kind. Notoriously difficult to raise from an egg, only the personal care of a dedicated IDLPO caretaker has allowed this baby to thrive. Imagine what would have happened if it had been sent to the Hub and forced to endure this cold and industrial system."

Judging by all the oohs and aahs, the whole delegation is falling in love with Shugly, just as we hoped.

"Maybe," Inaaya continues into the mike, "we should think carefully about whether this Hub really is the right move for the lost creatures of the multiverse."

I twist a knob on the control panel to zoom in on the delegates. We watch them conferring with Mrs

A, while Kaspar and Kaylar glance up at the camera in the room and whisper furiously to each other.

Mrs A stands up. Me, Modge and Inaaya hold our breath.

"Unfortunately, something has come up and the delegation has to leave now," Mrs Arburknuckle says.

"But you need to sign the contract!" Kaylar protests.

"We will need more time to consider, I'm afraid," Mrs A says as the delegates get to their feet.

In the control room, we all jump up and cheer.

"We did it!" Modge shouts.

"Yes!" says Inaaya, beaming like she's just won Mastermind.

"Take that, you rotten spider faces!" I yell. "Come on! Time to get out of here before they find us!"

Inaaya removes our memory stick from the computer. Modge tucks Shugly inside his shirt. And I'm about to turn off the video feed when suddenly everything goes black.

"Did you do that?" I ask Inaaya in the gloom.

"No."

"Power cut?" I suggest, hopefully.

"Maybe . . ." Inaaya agrees. But we're both scared it was something much, much worse.

None of us move. I can hear our hearts thumping in the silence.

Just before panic takes hold, the lights come on again and relief washes over me like a wave.

The video screens flicker, the meeting room cameras come on and my heart stutters. The delegates are all lying on the floor unconscious and wrapped up in webbing, which means –

The control room door slams open, Z'os in all his terrible, spidery glory stands there, rage filling his face. His mouth opens, revealing two wickedly sharp fangs dripping with venom.

There are no other doors, no windows, no escape. We're trapped.

"TIME TO DIE!" Z'os hisses and leaps into the room.

CHAPTER 27

We all scream and stumble backwards, terror burning in our blood as the monster attacks, lashing out with his legs, smashing screens and tables in rage.

With my plan in tatters, fear and panic swallow me up entirely. It's all I can do to dodge flying debris, sharp pincers and shooting web. I know we can't hold out for long.

A flying computer misses my head by inches and smashes into the wall, showering me in glass.

What was I thinking? How could three kids stop two evil spider monsters from taking over the world? They'll kill us, then use the serum to wipe the delegates' memories, and make them sign the contract anyway and we'll all be dead for nothing.

I search for Modge and Shugly and

find them cowering under a broken table. Where's Inaaya?

My cousin screams. I turn my head and see her trapped against the wall as Z'os rears back, ready to stab his fangs into her flesh.

"NO!" I scream, leaping forward – but I'm too late.

A long, thick tentacle has latched around Z'os' neck, yanking him backwards out of the room.

I look outside and see Mrs Arburknuckle wrestling with the spider monster. The bowl on her head must have protected her from the effects of the serum. Somehow she's escaped the webbing to come and rescue us.

"Run!" she screams at me as she wraps her tentacles around Z'os, holding him in place despite his furious struggles. "Get help!"

"Come on!" I call to Modge and Inaaya, and they follow me out of the room. I cast one last terrified look back at Mrs A.

"GO!" she yells again.

So the three of us pelt along the corridors, trying to reach the travel point, so we can get to Centralus and tell them what's happened. They'll save Mrs A and stop the J'effians from their evil plan. They have to.

But at the other end of the corridor Bee is emerging from her Kaylar skin. Those hairy legs creep over her chin one at a time and extend as they go. The crusty brown body expands to full-size like a puffer fish, the rock-like head wobbles on top with its five beady black eyes and that wicked slash of a mouth.

We skid to a halt, panic rising once again.

"We should have killed you all on the Nog dimension!" she croaks. "But you three have meddled your last. My venom will liquify your insides and soon there will be nothing left of you to find!"

"What do we do now, Danny?" Modge says.

"Yeah, got any more brilliant plans?" Inaaya asks.

I'm just waiting for Shugly to tell me I'm an idiot too when my eye lands on a thin copper pipe running along the wall, beneath one much larger silver pipe. Maybe I have got a plan after all.

"Distract her for a minute, will you?" I ask.

"A minute?" squeaks Modge.

"Well, as long as you can!"

Inaaya's hair is untangling, her socks are falling down and she's trembling with exhaustion but she nods at me, takes a deep breath, and steps forward, ready to take on the bullies despite everything."You J'effians are nothing but filthy scavengers! You destroy what others create for your own evil gain!"

"The J'effians are a great and noble race!" Bee argues back.

While Bee's distracted, I grab an empty fire bucket, run over to the pipes, find a joined bit and yank on the thin copper with all my weight. It bends slightly but doesn't break. I dig my grandad's multitool from my pocket and use the pliers to bend and cut through the metal.

"Enough of this, worthless human!" Bee yells, shooting a length of web at Inaaya, who dodges out of its way.

With one last cut, the pipe opens. I catch the brown powder that pours into the fire bucket. When it's full I bend the pipe back and start sawing at the silver pipe.

Inaaya dodges Bee's attacks once more, and then again. But the next time she slips and falls, and Bee leaps forward, ready to pounce.

Modge rushes to the rescue. "Get away from her, you crusty old monster!" he yells, stabbing at Bee's eye with a chewed-up pencil from his pocket.

Bee screams and lashes out, smashing Modge into the wall. He slithers down in a heap, one leg bent beneath him. My stomach drops but I keep hacking at the wide silver pipe until it's nearly open.

"Inaaya!" I shout.

Bee is still screaming. Startled out of her shock, Inaaya gets up and runs over to me. She takes one whiff of the fire-bucket contents and her eyes widen.

"Is this what I think it is?" she says.

I nod. "You know what to do!"

Bee is scrambling around the corridor, screeching and clawing at her damaged eye. She doesn't even notice Inaaya run up and tip the bucket of cleaning powder over her till it's too late.

"I WILL KILL YOU ALL!" Bee shouts, focusing on us once again.

I smash down on the larger, silvery pipe with my grandad's multitool and the metal breaks open. Thousands of beetles pour out. I have to bite my lip to stop from screaming when they run right over me. They're not interested in me though, or Inaaya, or Modge.

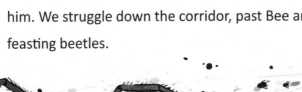

They head for Bee, swarming over her, desperate for the powder that covers her. She screams and struggles but in a moment there's nothing to see but a writhing mass as the beetles start to feed.

"Quick!" I order. "Let's go!"

Modge is unconscious and his leg's all twisted, so me and Inaaya grab one of his arms each and lift him. We struggle down the corridor, past Bee and the feasting beetles.

The travel station is in sight now. Somehow Inaaya and I find enough strength to carry Modge just that bit further. I can feel the comforting weight of my grandad's watch in my pocket, our ticket out of here, our chance to escape and get help –

But then Z'os jumps down from the ceiling, blocking our escape. A sharp spike of worry for Mrs Arburknuckle stabs my heart. Me and Inaaya sway on our feet, trying to hold Modge up, trying to catch our breath, trying not to give up even though everything seems impossible.

"Did you really think you could stop us?" Z'os hisses. "We've been planning this for YEARS! Three pitiful children are no match for the mighty J'effians!"

"How about three pitiful children and a veterinarian?" Dr Triffle Iffle says, appearing by our side.

"What are you doing here, you fool?" Z'os demands.

"What I should have done long ago!" the small vet shouts.

He points a Freeziflea canister at his employer. I feel a tiny glimmer of hope that we might actually survive, but one of Z'os' legs sweeps Dr Triffle Iffle's feet out from under him and he stumbles and falls, dropping the precious canister on to the floor.

Z'os laughs and quickly wraps the vet in webbing. "You see? Nothing and nobody will stop us!" he shouts. "The multiverse will be ours!"

He keeps laughing in evil triumph. Some sort of fire starts to burn in my belly.

I can't let them win. I won't.

I pass Modge to Inaaya and make a dive for the canister on the ground. Z'os spots me and shoots a net of web. Just before it covers me, I manage to grab the canister and throw it at Inaaya. She catches it – but drops Modge at the same time.

Z'os sees the danger at once and shoots a web line around Inaaya's wrist. He pulls on it hard and the canister falls from her hand, on to the unconscious Modge. The J'effian closes in on us, cackling and gloating. The end is near and I can't even move out of his way.

But then I spot something. Z'os is too busy enjoying his triumph to notice it too.

Shugly has emerged from Modge's shirt and is

licking his face with his little purple tongue. Modge twitches, then opens his eyes. He takes in the situation with one quick terrified glance, reaches for the Freeziflea canister, lifts – and fires.

I watch in amazement as he shoots with perfect aim.

"NO!" Z'os screams.

The Freezifleas hit and spread a thick white frost across his crusty brown skin in an instant. He stops dead, frozen to the spot.

The three of us are still staring in shock at the grotesque spidery statue when a horde of Centralus special agents arrive through the travel station, pointing weapons and shouting orders.

CHAPTER 28

After Dr Triffle Iffle has been dewebbed and calmed down enough to talk again, he reveals that he had called for help from Centralus after the delegates were attacked. The agents search the Hub and find his family for him and there's much squeaking and tail wagging when they're all reunited.

They also find Mrs A with her tentacles in a knot and her temper in a boil. She'd managed to dissolve the webbing used by the J'effians with her squid ink, but needed some help untangling her many appendages.

Once she's back to normal, she tells the agents that we saved the entire multiverse, which is pretty cool but not as cool as the agents themselves. They look like they'd be able to sort out anything, even rampaging spider monsters. They're a mix of species, but they're all wearing fancy silver and red uniforms that have REAL force fields they can activate and a host of impressive weaponry hanging from their utility belts.

Their leader, Agent Perflin Quen Moodle, is a W'elfen, which is a bit like an elf but better, apparently. She's about my size but her skin has green and gold markings, and her silver hair waves in the air and glows as she talks.

"You've done the multiverse a great service," she says to us in a bell-like voice as Bee (looking more like a freshly plucked chicken than a terrifying monster after her run in with the beetles) and her frozen brother are quickly locked into some sort of electrified sphere and transported back to Centralus HQ for processing. "I'll be recommending you all for a special service award."

"Cool!" Modge says as they heave him on to a stretcher to get his leg looked at. "Shugly should get one too, though."

"Bravery must always be rewarded," Agent Moodle agrees.

"Can I get one of them guns too?" Modge asks, pointing at her big shiny laser gun.

"No, you cannot!" Mrs Arburknuckle says. "No more danger for any of you! Ever! I can't take the stress."

"But danger is cool!" Modge insists as they wheel him away.

"Your friend is completely nuts," Inaaya says to me, shaking her head. "You do know that, right?"

"He's your mate too now," I remind her. "We both are."

Inaaya sighs and rolls her eyes but she can't quite hide her smile.

The look on my grandad's face when he steps out of my dad's car and sees half the estate gathered in the playground is amazing. I don't rush over though. I let everyone else surround him and sneak through the crowd to the car.

"Mum!" I call as soon as she gets out of the back seat.

"Danny!" She drops her bag and beams at me and I throw myself into her arms. I let her squeeze me for ages and ages as well, before I pretend to get annoyed and wriggle away.

"Look, Mum, there's a whole party for Grandad!" I tell her.

"I know!" she says in delight. "Dad told me you organised it. It all looks amazing."

I grin. "Everyone missed him so much."

"Well, he's back now. He just needs to take things easy for a while, not work so much."

"That's all right, Mum," I say. "I can help him."

Mum puts her arm around my shoulders and kisses my head. "You're a good boy, Danny. I missed you."

"I missed you too," I say. "I even missed your shepherd's pie!"

"Oi! Cheek!" She shoulders me away and grabs her bag. "Go and join the party. I'm going home to unpack and I'll see you later for a proper catch-up! I want to hear everything!"

I'm not sure she does, to be honest.

I find my grandad sitting on an old armchair that someone has dragged into the playground just for him, smiling as he watches everyone enjoy the party.

"Welcome Home Douglas."

"Danny! There you are! Come over here!" he calls out when he sees me.

I bend down to hug him. He feels good. A bit thinner but his arms still make me feel safe.

"It's good to see you," he says as I sit down on the arm of his chair.

"You too." I've already told him what happened at the IDLPO. Dad took me to visit the hospital last week, and while he and Mum had lunch together I told Grandad everything. He didn't have time to say much before the nurse came in, and then Mum and Dad came back. "I'm really glad you're home. Everyone missed you."

He looks around at all the people gathered together to welcome him home. "It's good to be home at last," he says.

"I'm so sorry," I blurt out, unable to keep the guilt in any longer.

Grandad smiles. "What are you sorry for?"

"I should have helped you more. It was all my fault you had a heart attack!" The relief of confessing at last makes my eyes prickle.

My grandad shakes his head. "No, Danny, it wasn't."

"But I was late and you had to do all that work on your own –"

"Danny, listen." He grabs my hand and holds it. "I had a heart attack because there was a blockage in my artery. It was nothing to do with you."

I sniff. "Really?"

"Really. You saved my life AND the whole multiverse, from what I've heard! Thank you."

It's like I can finally fill my lungs again without the weight of guilt pressing on my chest.

"That's all right, Grandad," I say. "I'd do anything for you."

Grandad smiles at me. "I'm a lucky man to have such a brave and brilliant grandson."

"Are you really going to be all right now?" I check.

"The doctors think I'll be fine, as long as I take it easy for a while."

"Me and Modge and Inaaya can help you a bit, if you want. I couldn't have done any of this without them."

Grandad grins. "Sounds to me like you and your friends can run the whole place better than me!"

"Never!"

"Well, maybe one day. IDLPO caretakers often run in families, you know?" He raises his eyebrows at me.

"Really?"

"Yep. And I bet Centralus would love to have you. You've already saved the whole darn multiverse and you're only ten! Imagine what you can do when you're grown up! I always knew you had it in you. I'm so proud of you, Danny."

A weird feeling sits inside me. It might be pride. Or hope. Or ambition even. I'm not really sure, but

I decide to ignore it for now and just see what happens.

"You knew there was something wrong though, Grandad, before anyone else even suspected," I say. "Did you know what Kaspar and Kaylar Arachnus were all along?"

My grandad shakes his head. "I just never could trust anyone that smiled that much!" he says and I laugh. "What was decided about those monsters in the end?"

The trial has only just finished. Mrs Arburknuckle came by yesterday to let me know the outcome.

"They're going to find a small dead planet and leave them trapped in a dimension fragment along with their henchman, Echelon Xanadu," I tell him. "They'll never escape and they'll never be found."

Grandad nods. "That sounds fair. What about the Hub?"

I shrug. "They've closed it for now. It's all back to normal at the IDLPOs. Some of the J'effian technology was pretty amazing though. Inaaya's already sent a whole folder full of ideas to Mrs A on how to integrate them into our system."

"I look forward to catching up on all of it!" Grandad says with a smile . "Now, this is supposed to be a party! Go off and find your friends and I'll tuck into some of these delicious sandwiches. I'm half-starved after all that hospital food."

It takes me ages to cross the playground. Everyone wants me to stop and have a chat, except for Sags and Keylon. When they see me coming, they shoot panicked looks at each other and duck behind the climbing frame. I guess they still believe me and Modge beat them up. EXCELLENT!

I eventually find Inaaya at the buffet table, filling up two plates with sausage rolls and samosas and crisps.

"Is your grandad enjoying the party?" she asks.

"Yeah. He looks good, doesn't he?"

I point to him and Inaaya smiles and waves. Grandad waves back. I grab a plate and pile it high, and follow Inaaya back to Modge's table.

"What took you so long?" he demands, snatching the plate and attacking the food like a starving wolf.

"Er, a thanks would be nice!" Inaaya snaps, sitting down next to him.

"I saved your life, Inaaya," Modge says, waving at the plaster cast on his leg. "The least you could do is make sure I don't starve."

Inaaya snorts. "I saved your life too!"

Modge looks at me. "Yeah, but I saved us all when it really mattered, right, Danny?"

"I think we all saved each other." I stuff a vegetable samosa in my mouth and chew.

"What did your grandad say?" Inaaya asks.

"He said he's got to take things easy for a while so I said we'd help him."

"Yes!" Modge says. "And he doesn't mind about Shugly?"

I look carefully at Modge and try to stay calm. "Have you decided then?"

Modge nods. "I told Dad I'm staying."

I try not to look too happy, but I am. I really don't know what I'd do if Modge wasn't around. But I know it's still hard for him.

"Because of Shugly?" I say.

"Well, he's part of the reason. Dr Triffle Iffle said Shugly has bonded with me. Like a chick and his mum. If I left he might not survive, so I have to stay really.

He needs me and obviously you lot couldn't manage without me neither." Modge's eyes are shining as he talks. I don't remember ever seeing him this happy.

"Ah, Mummy Modge, that's sweet, " I say, taking a swig of juice.

Inaaya laughs. "Mummy Modge! Suits you."

Modge rolls his eyes.

"Does your mum mind about you not going to live with her?" Inaaya asks.

Modge shrugs. "I think she understands. I promised to go and stay for a long holiday and see what it's like. You could come with me, Danny!"

"Cool!"

"I suppose you think I'll look after Shugly and help your grandad while you two go off on your hols?" Inaaya asks, eating some actual salad.

"Yeah, obviously!" I say because she definitely owes me. Her dad has got a new job in Birmingham but is being transferred to London in the summer. It was my idea that Inaaya stayed with us to finish her school term while her mum went to Birmingham, which was pretty genius of me.

Luckily, Inaaya's kind of grown on me. Without all

the family stress, she's actually quite fun sometimes. In fact, I might even miss her if she wasn't around. But DON'T tell her that.

"I do have a life, you know!" Inaaya says in a huff.

"Oh yeah, sorry. We forgot about Science Club!" Modge sniggers.

"I like Science Club!" Inaaya insists. "The other girls are really nice. It is pretty hard not to tell anyone there what I know though."

"Yeah," Modge sighs. "Really, we should be famous and on the news and stuff. I mean, if it wasn't for us we might all be living in a giant supermarket just waiting for everything to blow up!"

"But we're not," says Inaaya firmly. "Everything's fine again."

"For how long though?" Modge says.

I make a face. "Don't be daft. What else could possibly happen?"

Modge stares up at the sky. "Anything can happen, Danny. There's a whole multiverse out there, you know. And it needs us to look after it."

I grin at Modge. He might be a rubbish Avenger but he's MY rubbish Avenger and I'm keeping him.

"Go and get us some cake, Inaaya," Modge says. "I'm starving."

"I'm not your servant!"

"Er, hello! BROKEN LEG!"

"Shame it wasn't your mouth," she mutters.

I tune out their bickering and just enjoy having everything back to normal. Modge is right. Who knows how long it's going to last? With 3678920736 dimensions out there, anything is possible.

Anything at all.

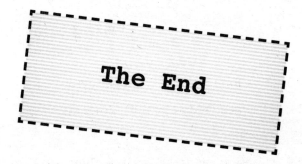

The End

Look out for . . .

INTERDIMENSIONAL EXPLORERS

book two, coming
soon to a multiverse
near you!

ACKNOWLEDGEMENTS

Enormous thanks must go first to my wondrous agent and friend Kate Shaw, who never gave up on me or this book.

Many thanks to Lindsey and Sarah and Lucy and Aleena and everyone at Farshore who have welcomed me and worked so hard to make this book shine.

To Ryan for his awesome design skills and to Jo for her amazing illustrations on the cover and throughout, THANK YOU!

To all my writer friends who support me, keep me sane, make me laugh and generally make this whole writing lark a joy – BIG SQUISHY HUGS TO YOU ALL.

For my lovely mum (and in memory of my brilliant dad) enormous thanks for giving me such a wonderful childhood and all the encouragement to chase my dreams.

And to Steve and Luke, many thanks for looking after me, putting up with me and providing food, hugs and inspiration – Love you loads xxx

LORRAINE GREGORY

Lorraine is the daughter of an Austrian mother and an Indian father and was raised on an East London Council Estate. She's had various jobs over the years including school dinner lady, chef and restaurant manager but secretly she always wanted to be a writer.

Lorraine loved creating *Interdimensional Explorers* because she got to dream up unlikely heroes who fight off evil aliens, travel between worlds and have a lot of fun (and a lot of snacks) trying to save the multiverse!

JO LINDLEY

is a children's book author and illustrator, living in Cardiff. At university, Jo replaced art with architecture, and her drawing became progressively more technical until one happy afternoon she rediscovered the joy of creating characters. She hasn't stopped since and now is a self-styled 'archistrator' (architect + illustrator).